S0-GQE-593

Crowley's Ridge

Collected Stories
by
H. R. Williams

Treble Heart Books

Crowley's Ridge
(Collected Stories)
Copyright © 2011 by H.R. Williams
All Rights reserved.

Printed and published in the United States
by Treble Heart Books
http://www.trebleheartbooks.com

Layout
Copyright © 2011 by Lee Emory
Cover Artist : Nancy LaFarra Wilson
All rights reserved.

The characters and events in this book are fictional, and any resemblance to persons, whether living or dead, is strictly coincidental.

All rights reserved. No part of this book may be reproduced or transmitted in any form, by any means, electronic or mechanical, including photocopying, recording, scanning to a computer disk, or by any informational storage and retrieval system, without express permission in writing from the publisher.

ISBN: 978-1-936127-45-0
ISBN: 1-936127-45-8
LCCN: 2011927128

Table of Contents

IN THE BEGINNING..6
    The Dog Run House..7

CROWLEY'S RIDGE AND THE NEARBY GROUND....9
    Boss Daniels..10
    Golden..23
    The Price of Ginseng..30
    The Visitor...35
    The Legend of Shaker Mose 51
    Glenda..57
    The Golf Match..61
    Storm Creek Lake...68
    Paddy's Peaches...80
    Mexicans..93
    Farewell, Tennessee...107
    The Ridge and the Town....................................117
    Charlie and Janet..129

LITTLEMYSTERIES...132
    Abigail and the Horse...133
    Black-Eyed Peas...139
    The Last Day of February...................................144
    Just Cause...149
    I Can't Get it Out of My Head............................154
    The New Line...158
    Time Will Tell..163

Table of Contents

Continued

SCARY STORIES..168
    The Children's Orchard...169
    There's a Basement in the Arcade......................179

GREAT OUTDOORS...187
    Bushytails...188
    Across the Levee..193
    Jugging with Bubba..199
    Shanging..205
    The Tom...210
    The Dangerous Relative.......................................216
    The Hunter...221
    The Trotline...226
    Jump...235
    The Trapper...240
    The Deer Stand...245

AT THE END..255
    Supper for the Dead..256

ABOUT THE AUTHOR..261

Dedication

To Tootie.
She is my firm foundation.

IN THE BEGINNING

"And all the loveliest things there be,
Come simply, so it seems to me."
Edna St. Vincent Millay

The Dog Run House

I lived as a child in a dog run house, which sat in the midst of a cotton field. A dirt road led up to it and cotton grew all around it. Rooms were set on either side and a center passageway, open to the weather, ran from the front to the back. That was called *the dog run* because dogs could run through it, and I could, too, when I was a child.

In the springtime, I'd lie on the dog run's wood-planked floor, watching men and mules turning the rich soil with plows and smoothing the dirt out with harrows and setting up rows for planting. A warm wind would drift over the newly turned ground and bring its fecund smell along and I'd turn my head from where I lay and watch blackbirds swarm and swoop over the dark earth and pluck fat worms from its surface.

Just beyond the field lay Crowley's Ridge, bringing its own special scent of rain-soaked woods and new growth, while all around I would here hear the distant sounds of wheeling birds and the farmer's "Giddyup, there" and the fluttering of soft breezes, wafting through the dog run.

In summertime, the cotton plants grew thick and tall and our house looked out on a green prairie. Autumn brought the killing frost, causing the leaves to shrivel and drop, and making the cotton bolls pop open so that the whole breadth of field became a white ocean for our dog run ship.

Day after day the people would come and pick the cotton, stuffing it into nine foot sacks that trailed along behind them. Wagons stood about the field, waiting for the sacks to be emptied, and the sacks would be emptied into them again and again until the fluffy white stuff flowed over the wagon's side.

Winter offered an empty and desolate view from our dog run house. Only thin, bare cotton stalks remained, catching the snow that blew along the ground and holding it in little clumps until the moaning wind swept it all away.

Lying in bed at night, I would listen to that wind swooshing through the dog run and pretend that I lived in a cave, high up in the mountains, where the wind was blowing across the face of a cliff. When I grew cold, I would pull the patchwork quilt up around my ears and imagine that I lay under the skin of a wild sheep.

Rain sometimes fell on our dog run house and its tin roof caught the echo of every drop, resounding like notes in a melody. And when the fall increased, that roof became an instrument of aqueous music. It was a lovely sound.

I should like to go back to that house, I think, and sit once again in the dog run. I would look out across the fertile fields and listen to the blackbirds keen and feel the warm, washing wind and soak all of it in, soak it all in and become a child again.

CROWLEY'S RIDGE AND THE NEARBY GROUND

"I am a part of all that I have met."
—Alfred, Lord Tennyson

Boss Daniels

Boss Daniels owned a farm on the east side of Crowley's Ridge and the working of it took up most of his days. He tended thirty acres of cotton and fifteen of corn. Six acres supported a peach orchard. His house, yard, and a pond, stocked with catfish, took up five acres. Woods covered all the rest, growing tall and dark behind the house and up a rising hillside.

The owner was part Cherokee and looked it, the flat, dark planes of his face highlighted by black eyes that reflected no light. His hair, combed straight back, grew thick and coarse and was the same color as a crow's wing. He moved deliberately and his walk was usually silent. It was an Indian walk.

Late one fall, Boss Daniels hitched two horses to his weathered wagon, loaded it with corn, and headed down the winding dirt road toward the village of LaGrange. The load was for Jack Barringer, who raised hogs on the outskirts of town. He regularly bought his feed from Boss.

Entering the town, Boss sat a little straighter. He removed his felt hat and used it to knock the dust from his pants and coat. A single dirt street led through the middle of LaGrange and he drove along it between the lined-up buildings. A few people stood on the wooden sidewalks. Most of them knew him and they waved as he passed. Boss gave each a solemn nod.

Cole Oglesby walked out the door of his grocery store and watched the wagon approach. "Howdy, Boss Man," he called. "You gonna stop back by?"

"Yep, be in later," Boss said, continuing down the street.

He'd known Cole since coming to Crowley's Ridge eleven years ago and had liked him from the start. Cole was straightforward and honest, and when Boss had needed credit the first few years, Cole granted it without hesitation. Cole knew his man. Boss Daniels would have killed himself trying to repay him. They were much alike, these two: steady and calm. A difference was that Cole liked to tilt the jug, tilted it frequently, and was sometimes the worse for it. Boss never drank, and Cole, who would have enjoyed having Boss as a drinking companion, took a peculiar comfort in that fact.

Boss drove on and watched the buildings pass by on either side. Most were constructed of rough or finished lumber. The Lee County Bank, a brick structure, appeared on the left. The First Baptist Church, also of brick, stood next door, so similar to its neighbor that local wags referred to them as the Lee County Church and the First Baptist Bank.

Down the street and on the right, past Sammie's Dress Shop and Harrington's Drug Store, stood LaGrange's other house of worship, the Church of God. Though far less imposing than it's counterpart, it boasted twice the membership. On Sunday and Wednesday nights soft organ music issued from the brick edifice, while loud singing, louder preaching, and a unique language, known as "speaking in tongues," burst from the other.

On towards the end of the street could be seen Darcy's Mule Barn, and across from it, Pennigar's Feed Store. On hot summer days the mule barn gave off a distinct and pungent odor.

A saloon called "Broadway" was the last structure Boss passed before leaving town. It was fashioned of gray lumber and sat on wooden piers so that you had to climb a flight of steps to reach the front porch. Boss had never been up those steps, but he'd been by Broadway on a Saturday night when its noise and music had made the clamor that came from the Church of God sound like the soft bleating of a shepherd's sheep.

Jack Barringer's place lay a quarter mile outside the town limits. Boss pulled into the yard and saw the owner staring down into one of his pigpens. He looked up at Boss and beckoned him over. Boss stopped his wagon beside Jack and got down. Called "Black Jack" by the townspeople, the man was a living symbol of his profession, as fat and filthy as any of his creatures. Boss wondered, not for the first time, if Barringer got his nickname simply because he had so much dirt on him.

"Hey, Boss, how're ye doin'?" Jack raised a grimy hand.

"Just fine, Jack. How are you?" Boss said in his formal way. The both stood watching a brood sow suckle her pigs.

"Same price as last time?" asked Jack, reaching into the hip pocket of his overalls.

"Same as always. Let's get it unloaded."

A short time later, Boss entered LaGrange again with an empty wagon. He hitched the team in front of Oglesby's and went inside. Cole Oglesby sat behind the counter working on a ledger. He looked up to see Boss standing in front of him.

"Never a sound," he grunted, looking his friend in the eye. "Never a sound. You're an Indian all right."

"Well, at least part," Boss said, examining the shelves behind the owner. "Cole, let me have a bag of that salt and about five pounds of pinto beans. Better give me another bag of flour, too."

"Right," Cole said, moving around and placing the items on the counter. "What else?"

"That'll be all," Boss said.

"When are you gonna get married and have some kids so I can sell you a real bill of groceries?"

"Never thought about it much."

"Well, you *oughta* think about it," Cole said. "You live by yourself up there much longer you're liable to go wild. You'll be coming into town with tusks growing out of your mouth, like some old wild boar."

"Might improve my looks," Boss said.

"Well, I guess you're human yet. That's the first time I ever heard you make anything like a joke." Cole bent over the counter a little way. "Listen," he said, "I want you to see something. It's settin' out back."

"What is it?"

"Come on. I'll show you," Cole said, leading the way out the rear door and onto the high back porch.

There below them sat a Model A Ford car, shiny and new and completely out of place in the shabby yard. It seemed almost alien in its surroundings, a gleaming black monument rising from the weeds.

Cole led the way down the stairs, walked over to the car, and trailed his fingers over the hood.

"Pretty, ain't it?" he said.

"Is it yours, Cole?"

"No, wish it was," Cole said, his eyes still fixed on the car. "It's my cousin's. She drove it up from Walnut Grove yesterday." He gave his friend a sideways look.

"It's Sara's, Boss. She's back for a visit."

The farmer stared at the storeowner with no change of expression on his face.

"She said she'd like to see you again."

Boss turned his broad back on Cole and climbed slowly up the steps. His mind was on a time, about a year and a half ago, when the hills were just turning green. He'd driven into town for supplies and met Sara in Oglesby's store. She'd come in with Oglesby's wife and Cole had said, "Boss, meet Sara Price. She's a cousin of mine." Sara had held out her hand to him and, after a moment, he'd taken it and they'd stood there, gravely looking at each other.

"Danged if she couldn't be *your* cousin," exclaimed Cole, staring at them both. "You look enough alike."

Boss could see what he meant. Sara's complexion was almost as dark as his and her ebony hair hung long and straight past her shoulders. The small, trim figure was very erect, and when she came toward him the movement had been as graceful as a dancer's. Boss remembered large, brown eyes under straight eyebrows and a face calm and serious. He'd thought it was a beautiful face.

"It'll be nice to see her again," he said, as they re-entered the store.

"Stick around for a few minutes and you can. She and the wife are coming over."

Bringing a bottle out from under the counter, Cole poured some whiskey in a shot glass. "Won't bother to offer you a drink," he said. "Gave up after the four hundredth time."

"Well, thanks anyway, Cole."

"Sara hasn't changed any," Cole said, bringing the glass to his lips. "Pretty as ever, if I do say so. Did you two ever get a chance to talk that day?"

"Some," Boss said. "She told me her husband had died of pneumonia and that she was part owner of a dress shop. Said she wasn't too happy doing that."

"Guess she wasn't. She sold her part about six months ago. What with the money from that and the husband's insurance, she don't have to worry about working. She still lives alone in that house they bought. I understand that's all paid for. What else she tell you?"

"She mentioned the house," Boss said. "I told her about my farm and she said—"

"Said what?"

"She said a farm was a world you could live in."

"What the devil she mean by that?" asked Cole.

"I think she meant that a house wasn't enough," Boss said.

"Yes, that's what she meant," came a soft voice from the open doorway.

Boss turned to look and thought it was Cole's wife who had spoken; she was in front. Then he knew that it came from the woman behind her. Sara stood outside the doorway and the setting sun cast a shadow before her. Cole was right.

Boss couldn't see any change except for interesting new hollows beneath the cheekbones. Sara wore a brown, full-length dress with a black cloth jacket over it. The raven hair hung full around her shoulders and she stood there like a dark promise for the coming night.

"How are you, Boss," she said, stepping around Mrs. Oglesby.

"I'm very well, Sara," he answered, looking into her face. He remembered all the times he'd summoned up that face in his mind. The image had always gladdened him.

Then, before he even thought about what he was doing, Boss found himself walking toward Sara. She held both hands out to him and he gave his willingly. They both stood looking at each other.

Mrs. Oglesby, a short, plump, and pleasant woman, stared at them with her mouth open and Boss could hear Cole's chuckle behind her.

"Don't look so surprised, Martha," he said. "Maybe they did more talking last time than we thought."

"No we didn't, Cole," Sara said, smiling. "You were in too much of a hurry to get me back to Walnut Grove. Maybe this time I'll stay a little longer."

Boss felt stunned as he continued to hold Sara's hands. He slowly released them and tried to take stock of himself. Sara was right. They really hadn't talked that much on the day they met, not much at all. Yet, just now, he'd almost run over to her and had grabbed her hands like a drowning man. And she had not withdrawn them, had stood close to him as she gazed into his eyes.

"Boss!" Martha Oglesby's voice brought him back to reality. "We saw your team out front and I told Sara I'd ask you; I need to stay and help Cole close the store. I wondered it you'd walk Sara back to our house. I didn't think you'd mind. She grinned and added, "Now, I'm sure of it."

"No, I don't mind," replied Boss and realized he was staring at Sara again. Something stirred within him and he felt light headed. "Are you ready to go?" he asked, and was relieved to hear that, at least, his voice was still steady.

"Yes, Boss," Sara replied, "and thank you."

Martha watched them descend the steps together and move off into the dusk. She turned to Cole and said in her mirthful way: "They oughta take somebody along to laugh for'em."

Her husband smiled and placed an arm around her shoulder. "You know," he said, "that might not be something they need."

Boss and Sara walked slowly down the darkening street, illuminated here and there by lanterns and lamps. The buildings on either side rose up vague and shadowy in the night. Most of the windows facing the street gave off a warm glow. Every once in a while, movement could be seen behind the panes, people stirring around or curtains being drawn against the outside traffic. The wind touched both their faces and brought the faint sound of fiddle music, drifting up from Broadway. Their footsteps made no sound in the soft dust.

"Boss, I want to ask you something," Sara said, slipping her arm around his. "What happened back there in the store?"

"You mean when I—"

"Yes, I mean that," she said.

"I don't know," Boss said in a low voice.

"I thought about you after I left. I knew you'd be back at your place and I'd think of you alone up there. I'd wonder what you were doing."

"Always the same thing, working the farm."

"Don't you have any help?"

"Sometimes I hire men to help me in the fields or to cut wood. Other times I work by myself."

"You do the housework, too?" she asked, giving him an impish smile.

"Yes," Boss said. "I generally do that at night."

He thought about that night work, deep darkness around the hillside house and spreading lamplight inside and the whisper of broom straw on a wooden floor, a lonely sound in an otherwise soundless room. He felt a tug on his arm and realized Sara had stopped and was looking up at him.

"Is Boss your real name? I've never heard you called anything else."

"No, it's John. But you're right, I can't remember the last time anyone called me that."

"Do you mind these questions, Boss? I just want to know things."

"I don't mind if you're the one that's asking."

"Where did *Boss* come from?"

"I guess it started with my daddy. He said that when I was a youngster all the other kids would stand around waiting for me to tell'em what to do, like I was the boss. He started calling me that and it stuck."

"Boss," said Sara, "What a strange name to give a child."

"Yes, I guess so," Boss said, and his mind flew back to an even stranger name for a boy, or any *man* who was white. He thought of the word, "Manoos" and the maternal grandmother who bestowed it. Small, dark, and wrinkled, gray hair hanging down her back in two long braids, black, gimlet eyes. Pure Indian. Pure *Cherokee* with Cherokee words on her withered lips.

"Manoos! You are Manoos," she would tell him. "It means 'manly one.' Yes, little man. You will be such a one. It is your secret name."

And Boss Daniels had not forgotten. Manoos was inside him, mixed in with his Indian blood and tribal memories of things he himself had never seen; a deer brought down with an arrow in its side, or a blazing campfire reflecting off tree trunks, or wild dancing under a cold moon.

"Boss?" Her questioning voice came to him. "Anything wrong?"

"No," he answered, "nothing's wrong."

They had stopped beneath a street lantern and its glow fell on Sara's face. Boss gazed into her dark eyes and felt a gentle release. He did not realize it was a lessening of his strange, wild loneliness. Sara reached up and placed her hand on his cheek. Boss kissed her then and was surprised at the softness of her parted lips. He drew her closer and felt her mouth moving against his, felt the heat and closeness of her body and her warm, sweet, breath on his face. One small hand reached around his neck and pulled him closer and Boss Daniels kissed her harder and deeper than before.

Finally, they drew apart and walked on, arm in arm, to Cole's house. Neither spoke until they reached the porch and Sara had turned to look at Boss again.

"Cole told me you'd be going back tonight," she said.

"I've got to. There's jobs I have to do first thing in the morning. They can't be put off."

"I know," she said, "feeding hungry animals among other things."

"That's right."

Sara looked steadily at him and her slender form straightened as she spoke. "I want to tell you something and

I want to speak plain. I have to. I don't know any other way."

Boss stood motionless before her.

"You have no way with words and I don't mind that, but something has got to be said before you leave. She paused before murmuring, "I won't forget tonight. It meant something to me. *You* mean something to me."

She gazed at Boss a moment longer, then started up the steps.

"Sara!" he called, as she reached the front door. "Sara, I..." And he couldn't say any more.

"Good night, John," she said, smiling down at him. Then she went inside and closed the door behind her.

Boss walked slowly back up the street toward his wagon. The lamps were still burning inside Oglesby's store, but when he reached the wagon, he climbed in and headed out of town. Soon, the lights of LaGrange disappeared behind him and he was swallowed up in darkness. The stars glimmered across a clear, moonless sky and outlined the hills on either side. Boss couldn't see the road ahead, but he trusted the horses to follow it. Their hooves made a soft clopping sound in the dirt and the old wagon gave off an occasional creak. The wind had turned chilly and he pulled the coat collar higher about his neck. All around, the vast forest lay hidden in the night.

Boss woke up the next morning and lay for a while in his bed. He'd slept later than usual and sunlight streamed in through an eastside window. He lay and watched some dust motes floating in a cascade of light. Finally, he got up, walked to the washbasin and splashed cold water on his face. He dried off with a clean towel and slipped on his work clothes. Sitting on the side of the bed, he put on his high-topped shoes and laced them up. All the time he was thinking about Sara.

It meant something to me, Boss. You mean something to me.

Yes, but how much? Enough to see him again? Enough to come up here? Could she leave a house in town with town friends and town streets to drive her new car on? And with a sinking feeling, it came to Boss how different their lives were. They were from different worlds.

It meant something to me, Boss. You mean something to me.

He remembered the look on Sara's face when she'd said those words and he suddenly felt ashamed. She was her own woman. He knew that, and he knew whatever her decisions were, they would never be influenced by towns or friends or a place to drive her car.

And another thing he knew. Somehow he had turned a corner. Whether anything ever came of it or not, he would be forever changed by his encounter with this woman. Because of Sara, he had moved outside himself.

Boss Daniels got up, squared his shoulders, and walked out the front door. Cecil Howard, one of the hired men, was hitching the mules to a plow. He already knew which field to work and was about to go there without saying anything to Boss, who was standing in the yard. Boss seldom spoke to him, except to deliver instructions. He'd gotten used to this and was surprised to look up and see the owner walking toward him.

"Hello, Cecil. How are you this morning?"

It was a moment before the worker could collect his thoughts, but then he said: "Doin' fine, Mr. Daniels."

"Well, I know you're anxious to get that ten acres finished, so I won't keep you. You've got some pretty weather for it."

Cecil Howard just stared at Boss with his mouth slightly open. One of the reins hung loose in his hand.

Just then, a faint noise reached them from the bottom of the hill and they both looked down at the winding dirt road. It lay behind a line of oaks, but its dusty surface could be glimpsed here and there between the giant tree trunks. That was where the throbbing sound came from and it grew louder as they listened. Something was coming up the road.

An object passed between two of the trees. It vanished for a moment, and then came into full view and started up the hill toward them. The Model A Ford and the hair of the woman who drove it were black, very black in the morning light.

Boss watched the car approach and a huge smile settled across his face. He closed his eyes for a long moment, and then opened them to a world that was clean and fresh and full of promise.

Golden

When I was six, pneumonia paid a fatal visit on my mother and father and left me an orphan. My grandparents took me in and I spent my childhood with them on their farm. Lucius Johnson and my grandmother, Janie, were up in years but both were healthy and active. Grandpa needed to be. On him depended the continuing success of his holdings, which consisted of cotton, corn, hogs, and about fifty head of cattle.

I can see him still, a striking man with a full head of steel gray hair, and eyes, black as anthracite, set deep in their sockets. My grandmother was small and quick and full of mirth. It seemed she was always cooking and most of her time was spent in the kitchen. It was there my grandfather led me on the day he brought me home.

"I'm going to have to fatten you up, young man," she exclaimed, running her fingers over my ribs. "You're thin as a rail."

"Might as well start right now," said grandpa as he headed for the door. "And tomorrow you can pack him a big lunch."

"What for," asked grandma, looking quickly to her husband.

"That's when he starts to school."

And so I did and my days soon fell into a set routine: school every weekday and small chores in the late afternoons, but most of the weekends free to do whatever I pleased. Three other families lived on grandpa's place. The parents worked for him and their children became my playmates on the farm. And there *was* one other companion. That was grandpa's dog.

His name was Golden and when you saw him you knew that no other name could fit as well. His sleek coat looked just like that precious metal, glowing and shining under the sun. A huge dog, Golden moved with the pride and grace of something never quite domesticated, a breed apart from the usual canine world. But my grandfather had owned him from a pup and he was nothing else but Lucius's dog. He'd allow a bit of play out in our big front yard, but if Lucius appeared, Golden would stop and silently stare at him, waiting for a command to be issued, poised for instant obedience.

Lucius had trained him for a cattle dog and swore he'd never seen a better one. I'd watch them coming home at sunset, bringing a herd of cattle, and the animals would be so tightly bunched you'd think they had a rope around them. The old man would be walking off to one side and his dog would drift right and left behind the herd, keeping them moving, keeping them *controlled.* Occasionally, a cow would break off and go scampering to one side and you'd hear the old man yell, "HAAAAHHH GOLDEN " and point to the offender, but by then a flash of amber had appeared on the other side of the creature and brought her back into line.

Rufus Steinbeck, a neighboring farmer, watched this performance one afternoon and when grandpa came up to the house, Steinbeck was waiting.

"Loosh, what'll you take for that dog," he asked in his habitual growl.

Grandpa gazed at him for a moment. "Nothing," he replied.

"Oh, I'll just take him on along, then."

"You know what I mean, Rufus" said grandpa. "He can't be bought at any price. Just put it out of your mind."

Golden, meanwhile, stood in front of the two men, swinging his head from one to the other as they talked.

"Hah Golden," the old man ordered, pointing toward the front porch, "go to the house."

The dog headed across the yard and up the porch steps. He turned around before the front door and lay down with his head resting on his paws. The alert, intelligent eyes were fixed on the old man.

Rufus stared at the dog and slowly nodded his head. Then, he showed his tobacco stained teeth in a smile and said, "Well, let me know when you reach a final decision?"

"You just heard it," the old man replied, smiling in return.

That decision saved my life.

For as long as anyone could remember, wild hogs had roamed the hills and gorges of Crowley's Ridge. In the beginning, ordinary domestic swine had wandered into the surrounding wood and remained there, becoming feral things, foraging and breeding in the wilderness. After a few generations, the offspring looked nothing like their forebears. These creatures were truly wild, with lean hard bodies and elongated snouts. Curved, sharp tusks protruded from their lower jaw and they could disembowel a larger animal with one vicious swipe. Always hostile, they would attack without provocation. They feared man not at all. Grandpa said it was because they'd been acquainted with men previously. He often hunted them because they were a danger to domestic stock. Any dogs taken along on these hunts were judged to be expendable. No dog alive was a match for those slashing tusks.

On a Saturday morning in late October, after finishing breakfast with my grandparents, I asked if I could go down to Bear Creek and fish off the bank. Grandpa said yes, but first I needed to carry some water to the hogs. I went out to the pump with a metal bucket in each hand. The pump handle was too high to reach, but grandpa had placed a box for me to stand on. I filled the small buckets and carried them over to the hog pen. I was about to open the gate, but halted and froze instead.

Something was wrong.

The pen held three sows. Two had litters of small pigs and the third was waiting to be bred to the next available boar. Usually, when I came with water or slop, they'd squeal and mill around and push against the gate. This time, though, they were all huddled against the left fence and they weren't making a sound, not even the baby pigs. They weren't moving either. Then, from the opposite side of the pen, I heard a crash and the splintering of wood. Whatever made the noise was outside the fence and around the corner and I couldn't get a glimpse of it. Slowly, with hammering heart, I started forward with the pails of water still clutched in my hands.

I reached the corner and stepped around it.

The huge, wild boar was busy trying to beak through the fence and get to the brood sow. He thrust his narrow, bony snout under the bottom railing and jerked it upward, causing the pine wood to split and fly apart. Two dingy tusks rose from each side of the bottom jaw and ended in sharp points just above the flared nostrils. He was looking into the pen, but suddenly he swung his head around and both inflamed eyes were boring into *me*.

Instantly, he lowered that head and charged.

For a second, I stood transfixed before his deadly attack. Then, I dropped the pails, turned, and ran toward the house. I heard a clang behind me and glanced back to see one of the pails, sailing end over end with water spraying from it in a glistening fan. The boar had slowed, for a moment, to hit the pail, but now he was on me again.

He never made a sound but I could hear the three sows squealing in terror. I ran as I had never run before but I knew that it was hopeless. He was too fast for me. I could hear him right behind me and I felt his hot breath on my bare ankles. Suddenly, a flash of pain ripped across the back of my leg as he slashed me with a tusk. I screamed and tried to run faster and looked ahead in bug-eyed terror at the home I would never reach.

And then it happened.

My grandfather appeared on the front porch, followed by a dog that could not be bought at any price. He stared at the scene before him, and then, like an avenging prophet, he stretched out his long right arm toward the monster behind me.

And his voice sounded as a bugle in the face of my fear:

"Haaaahhh, Golden"

The great dog bounded forward and sprang off the porch, sailing through the air toward me, and then he was on the ground and coming like a tawny streak. I saw that broad head with the ears laid back and the white fangs bared and I heard the rumbling growl come from deep in his throat, and as my grandpa's dog rose once more into the air, I thought for a fearful moment that he had come for me.

I screamed and threw myself forward and felt the wind from Golden's passing.

From behind me, I heard the whump of bodies colliding and the shrill cry of the boar. My lips twitched in a smile, just before I passed out, because I recognized it as a squeal of pain.

Later that morning, I awoke with some pain of my own. Grandpa had laid me on the couch and grandma was holding a cup of hot tea under my nose. The pain came from my right leg and I looked down to see it wrapped in a bandage.

"You're all right," she said, handing the cup to her husband and placing a cool palm on my forehead. "The cut wasn't deep. I put some disinfectant on it, but you keep that bandage on for awhile."

She went back to the kitchen and Grandpa held the tea to my lips. I took a deep swallow and felt the warm liquid go all the way to my stomach.

Grandpa smiled at me and said, "You had a close call." Then he got that black-eyed, grim look and murmured, "I called the dog off and the boar ran away. Maybe I'll meet him again sometime."

I stared up at him and asked, "Grandpa, where's your dog?"

"Why right here," answered the old man as he got up and swung the front door back.

Morning sunlight streamed through the opening, lighting up a golden presence in the center. Grandpa's dog padded into the room and stood close by my side, looking at me. I threw both arms around him and buried my face in his neck and kept it there for a long time, while sob after sob racked my body.

Finally, I sank back down on the couch. The great dog remained motionless and silent. Seeing the questioning look in his eyes, I slowly nodded my head. Then, Golden turned and trotted through the doorway, following his master who'd gone out before him.

The Price of Ginseng

The old man lay flat on his back in a small defile and squinted into the sun. He spread his arms to either side, feeling the ground rise under each hand. Raising his head, he caught sight of the dead rattlesnake (the one that had bitten him) stretched just beyond his feet. I shouldn't have wasted so much strength killing the snake, he thought. There are thousands of snakes in these hills. What's this one, more or less? This is the one that bit you, that's what. And so he had killed him. The old man had always given measure for measure and there'd really been no question about killing the snake.

His right hand touched a cloth bag, lying at his side. He lifted the bag up and a batch of ginseng roots rolled out onto his stomach. Their fantastic shapes reminded the old man of a bulbous menagerie with a few man-shapes mixed in. That was the nature of ginseng with its roots gnarled and twisted into a multitude of forms. Those shaped like men were the most valuable, believed by the Chinese to banish impotency. When his brothers were alive, they had hunted the ginseng all over these hills, hunted it and sold it as a part of their living, another way of surviving.

In the beginning, there was the mother and father and the four sons. Then, when Lloyd the oldest was twelve, pneumonia struck down the parents and left the brothers orphans. An instinct within them seemed to whisper: *If you stick together, you may survive, but separately you will perish.* All of them had heeded that whispering voice and they had depended on each other until only the Ginseng Hunter remained. Now he lay unaided and helpless in the depths of Crowley's Ridge.

They had all spent their boyhood in these hills. Lying there, the old man seemed to sense his brothers presence, and in his loneliness felt like crying out to them. Had they ever dug ginseng in this part of the Ridge? Probably. Likely they had wandered down this very draw. Ginseng was a rare plant, difficult to locate, and they had searched everywhere for it.

And it was dangerous to look for on account of the snakes. Rattlesnakes seemed to have an affinity for it. In the heat of summer, they loved to coil up in its shade. The brothers were constantly on the lookout for each other. If one of them wandered into a clump of ginseng plants without checking it first, the rest would be on him in an instant, chiding and scolding. As with all children, they mixed play with everything, but there was no playing when it came to the snakes.

The Ginseng Hunter's left arm stretched lifeless on the

ground and appeared to belong to another man, a very fat man. The swelling had come on fast and he couldn't move the arm. He could feel it, though. The pain throbbed through the puffed flesh so fiercely, a lesser man might have yelled. But the old man did not yell or even moan. He had suffered much in his eighty-four years and had learned to endure. On this trip he'd brought neither knife nor snakebite kit. He didn't know why he'd neglected to bring them. There were many precautions he no longer took. Well, you should have taken this one, the old man thought, because now you are likely to die.

He shook his head and closed his eyes against the gleaming sky. And to take some of his mind from the pain, he thought of the previous hours. He'd arisen early, out of habit, and drank his coffee alone, out of necessity, his wife in her grave these many years. His old rusted-out pickup had carried him from his house in LaGrange into the neighboring hills of Crowley's Ridge. The old man though how pleasant the drive had been, how the ridges shone in early morning light and he remembered the hollows, shadowy and cool in their depths. His lips turned down at the corners. Yes, he thought, very pleasant. You were mobile then, instead of flat on your back, and there was no pain and no rattlesnake venom coursing through your veins.

He'd parked his truck at the entrance to a dirt trail and followed it on foot into the forest. "They'll find the truck," he said aloud. "They'll know where to look for me."

Yes, and how many hills have you walked over and how many hollows have you traveled through since you left that truck. Fool, he thought, you'll be dead before anyone misses you. And when they *do* come to look, they'll get lost in this place a dozen times over before they find your body. They would not be like him. No matter how far away he got or how many twists and turns he took, he could always come straight back to his truck. He was never lost in the woods and he'd always supposed it was a gift.

Gradually, the old man became aware of a lessening in his pain. He was afraid to believe it, at first, but undeniably the pain had lessened. He took a deep breath and the pain left him completely. He lay very quietly so as not to re-awaken it. A soft wind ruffled through the hollow and murmured in his ears and the murmuring sounded like voices, the comforting and familiar voices of brothers.

They had given each other nicknames. Lloyd had once owned a blacksmith shop, so he became "Hoss." Aubrey, the youngest, because of a stooped posture and a shambling gait, was called "Humpy." Gene, the next to oldest, always wore his pants high on the hips. He became "Highpockets," later shortened to "Pockets." The Ginseng Hunter had served a couple of years as a young deputy, so he ceased to be Ray and was called "Cop." And these became their secret names.

Hoss, swaggering, boastful Hoss, with an exuberant spirit that lifted them all and gave them strength. He'd married four times, and after the last nuptial had moved the bride's widowed mama in with them, proclaiming to his amused brothers that he had garnered not only a mother-in-law, but a *mother*, he who held the most vivid memory of a real mother of long ago.

And Pockets, the leader. He of the meticulous dress and cultivated air and a quiet aura of competence had little formal education, none of them did, but he finally rose to manage a great plantation at the southern end of Crowley's Ridge.

Humpy was the youngest and so under the other's special protection until he died in his thirties. Humpy, the quiet and inoffensive one, the one who was always hungry. Humpy, the true orphan.

And me, thought the old man. Cop, the survivor.

Hoss dead of cirrhosis, caused by too much drink. Pockets struck down by a shattering heart attack. Humpy, shot in the woods by some fool of a hunter, who mistook him for a deer. And Cop, the survivor, going on without them. The old man took a deep breath and closed his eyes.

He awakened to the cry of a night bird and saw the sun sliding behind a distant ridge. A final swath of crimson light lay across his stomach and lit up the roots of ginseng. The Ginseng Hunter stared at the myriad shapes and focused on three of the man-forms. They really were shaped liked human figures, and to the old man, gazing at them with shadowed eyes, they came to resemble the brothers. Cop smiled at them and touched them with his good hand and whispered out to each of them their secret names.

His final breath was only an added whisper.

The sun sank below the earth and the following darkness filled the hollow first, covering up the old man and the snake and the scattered roots of ginseng. Then the darkness rose to the hilltops and spread over the highest trees and finally lay across the whole length of Crowley's Ridge.

The watchful night bird called again and kept calling into the silence.

The Visitor

It was a Saturday morning and Mr. Cole Beatty was talking to my daddy and the rest of the farmhands. "Boys," he said, "I know y'all have already heard about our visitor. Now, his name is Robert Rumsfeld, and a'course he's from England. He'll be here for one day only to look at my crops. Mr. Rumsfeld owns two textile mills and he wants to check the quality of our cotton. If he likes what he sees, he'll buy, and that can't do anything but help the country."

"And help Beatty Farms," put in Sam, a long, lanky tractor driver.

"Well," said Mr. Cole, looking out over the men, "last time I checked, Beatty Farms was a part of the USA."

"Hey Cole," said Woodrow Beatty, Cole's brother and the farm mechanic, "whereabouts in England is Rumsfeld from?"

"How the hell do I know, Woody," said Mr. Cole, letting them glimpse a flash of his famous temper. "Rumple Dumple on

Chimes. Does that satisfy you? Now, his valet will be with him and—"

"His what?" said Sam.

"His damn valet, Sam. Are you too ignorant to know what a damn valet is?"

"Well heck, Cole, I never even heard the *word* before."

Mr. Cole was about to lose it, but he took a deep breath and reined that temper in. I was a little disappointed, because I always enjoyed watching him blow up. All it ever amounted to was a lot of cussing and hollering, and when the storm was over, he was as meek and mild as one of his milk cows.

"A valet," he said, "is a fellow that goes around with an upper class Englishman and tends to his needs."

Now if the farm harbored someone who might be called the "farm character," or sometimes the "farm drunk," that someone would be Jesse Potts, who looked after the cattle. He stood waving his hand in the air like a schoolboy in class. Mr. Cole sighed and said, "You got a question, Jesse?"

"What kinda needs?"

Kaboom! The volcano finally blew. "*Any* kinda needs, you country clown. If the Englishman wants his bath drawed, that's a need. If he wants his clothes laid out, that's a need. Hell, for all I know, if he wants his ass wiped, that's a need. Now, I gotta need myself. I *neeeed* for you yahoos to stick to the subject."

The boss took a deep breath and started in again. "Now, Mr. Rumsfeld will come in on the nine o'clock train. I'll drive to the station in my car and I want y'all to follow me in the pickup. Raymond," he said, pointing to my daddy. "you drive the pickup. When we get to the station, I want you to park right behind me. Sam, you, Woodrow, and Jesse, get out and stand alongside the truck. Now, this Englishman is what you called real reserved, so I'll be the only one to speak to him."

"Dang, Cole," said Sam, hitching his pants up over protruding hip bones. "Ain't you goin' a little overboard with this thing?"

I expected another eruption, but Mr. Cole just gave the thin man a gentle smile.

"Sam," he said, "you got to understand that it's what this man expects. Why back in England, that's regular treatment for him. And by God, that's the way he's gonna be treated over here, so he'll go back to his mills and order a train load of cotton from Beatty Farms, not to mention every other farmer in the Delta." Then he cast a glance my way and said, "You want to ride into town with me, Little Ray?"

I looked at my Daddy. He nodded his head and I made a dive for Mr. Cole's new Packard. I loved riding in that car. It was big and powerful, but whisper quiet on the road. And it had soft velvet seats. We headed down the highway.

Mr. Cole glanced at me and said, "Whaddaya been up to, short stuff?"

"Going to school, and helping my daddy in the evenings."

"You doin' okay in school?"

"Yessir, I make pretty good grades."

"Well, keep on doin' that," declared Mr. Cole.

"My teacher says I'm a real good reader."

"Hmmm. You ever read anything about England?"

"No, we're studying America now." I thought for a moment. "I checked *Robin Hood* out of the school library."

"That got something to do with England?"

"Yessir. Robin Hood lived there."

"What'd he do?"

"He lived in Sherwood Forest and him and his merry men robbed people."

"Dang! Robbed'em you say?"

"Yessir, but they only robbed rich people. Then they took the money and gave it to the poor."

"Well that don't make it right, Little Ray. Rich people got a right to their money, and I'll tell you something else. The world's lucky to have'em."

"Sir?"

"Well, looka here. What if somebody robbed me, took all my money. How do you suppose I could pay your daddy's salary, and everybody's else's salary on this place? Nope! I'm tellin' you the world needs rich people."

"Yessir."

"And by the way," he added, "when you're around our visitor, make sure you don't say nothin' about Robin Hood."

"No, sir, I won't."

"Good boy," said Mr. Cole.

Pretty soon we came up to the outskirts of Marianna. We headed down Main Street, then turned left and drew up beside the railway station. Me and Mr. Cole got out of the car and the men piled out of the pickup. We all stood looking down the length of railroad track, but there was no sign of the train. A cool breeze swept in from the west and ruffled my hair. I glanced in that direction and saw a low-lying cloud bank stretching all along the horizon. I could see it moving toward us, looking purple under the morning sun. The wind gusted stronger and I thought I heard the low rumble of thunder.

"Well, heck," said Mr. Cole, "a rain sure ain't gonna help anything."

Lightning darted from beneath the cloud and this time the thunder reached us in a booming crash. And in the quiet that followed, we all heard the train whistle. We looked northward to where the track curved out of sight, and around that curve came the train. The engine ground past the station, came to a stop, and sat there, chuffing smoke and letting off steam. The doors on the passenger cars opened and out came the riders, some holding luggage, some grasping small children, and all glancing up at the thundercloud. Then, a heavy-set man appeared at the door, stepped down to the pavement, and stood looking about him. Some of the passengers turned to stare, and I could understand why, because this fellow was something to look at. He wore a tan suit, with all the trimmings; that is to say a white shirt with cuffs and cufflinks showing at the wrists, a green vest, a bow tie, also green, and brown calf-length boots, shined real bright. Oh, he was a foreigner all right, everybody could tell that at a glance. And if they couldn't, they knew it as soon as the stranger opened his mouth and that English accent came out. He looked behind him and said: "Come along, Stevens, we haven't got all day."

And out the door came Stevens. He was a slim, trim little fellow, no more than five and a half feet tall, and holding onto a valise. He stepped up behind his boss, set his gear on the ground, and they both stood looking around them.

And then Mr. Cole went into action. He hurried up to them and stuck out his hand. "I reckon this is Mr. Rumsfeld," he said.

The Englishman took the boss's hand and gave a little bow. "That is correct, sir. And do I have the privilege of addressing Mr. Cole Beatty?"

"You sure do," he said, and just stood there grinning.

Mr. Rumsfeld gave a little cough and said, "Shall we proceed, Mr. Beatty?" Mr. Cole nodded, kept that grin going, and headed for the car. The Englishman followed, and Stevens sprang to the rear door and stood holding it open for his master.

Except now, Mr. Rumsfeld had stopped moving. He was just standing there, flat footed, with his mouth half open. And for some reason or other, he was staring straight at *me*. Finally, he got in the back seat and his servant joined Mr. Cole in the front. I got in the truck cab with my daddy and Sam climbed in beside me. Mr. Cole headed out of town and we followed close behind. I looked through the rear window at Jesse and Woodrow, sprawled in the bed of the pickup.

Both car and truck swept past the last house in Marianna, and all at once we were in the country. Cotton fields stretched out in every direction and the fluffy cotton, boiling out of its bolls, made all the fields look like acres of white foam. We turned right, onto a dirt road, and drove past a hand-made sign reading: "Beatty Farms." In the distance, I could see the Beatty house, a wooden two-story building, painted dark gray and standing among some elm trees. I expected Mr. Cole to turn off at the house but he kept right on going. We followed him down the road and deeper into the cotton fields.

A clap of thunder sounded and I turned my head to look out the rear window. The low-lying cloud was almost upon us and I could see rain slanting down from it and striking the western cotton fields. Jesse and Woodrow were busy unfurling a roll of tarpaulin. They laid it flat across the bed and got underneath. All I could see of them now was two formless lumps. I watched the rainfall come up from behind, spattering into the dusty road. Suddenly, the storm swept over us and my daddy turned on the windshield wipers.

The big Packard just kept plowing ahead. I figured Mr. Cole was hoping the rain would stop before the road got too muddy to navigate. Suddenly, the Packard's rear end sank into the mud and the car shuddered to a stop. My daddy came to a standstill behind the Packard and there we sat. The big car began to inch forward and back, forward and back, as Mr. Cole tried to rock it out of the mud hole. I couldn't see that he was making any progress. Then the driver's door opened and Mr. Cole got out and came splashing toward us.

"Okay boys," he yelled, "we're all gonna get at the back of the car and push her out of there."

"And who's gonna drive?" asked Woodrow, throwing back the tarpaulin.

"I asked Stevens to do it," said Mr. Cole.

As we approached the rear of the car, I could see that Stevens had already taken his place behind the wheel and was looking at us over his shoulder. At a signal from Mr. Cole, all six of us pressed together and placed our hands on the rear of the Packard. Mr. Cole lifted his face to the heavens and cried, "Give'er the gun, Mr. Stevens." At the same time, all of us gave a mighty shove. The engine went on idling and we straightened up to look at Stevens. He was staring at us with a confused look on his face.

"Mr. Cole," I said, "I don't think he understands what 'give'er the gun' means."

Our boss gave me a sort of fazed look and said, "Awright, get ready to push again." Once more, he looked heavenward and hollered, "Go, Mr. Stevens." And then, just for insurance, he yelled again: "Go, Stevens! Go."

On the second 'go' the engine roared and the big car lurched forward, only to settle once more into the mud. After three more, 'Go, Mr. Stevens' and three more heaves, the Packard seemed sunk as deep as ever. We all straightened up and stood there, heaving and panting. Mr. Cole sounded like a dying mule. He turned and plopped down on the rear bumper and Stevens 'give'er the gun'. The car made another lurch, Mr. Cole's feet flew out from under him, and he landed kersplat in the mud. "No, Mr. Stevens," he screamed, but it must have sounded like 'go' to Stevens, because he "give'er the gun" again. Mud spewed from under the rear wheels and covered Mr. Cole from head to toe.

And the rain kept pelting down.

My daddy helped the boss to his feet and the rest of us stood around, trying not to laugh. Stevens was looking over his shoulder, but the Englishman hadn't moved.

"Well," said the boss, "it ain't no use keeping this up. I want you all to take the truck back to the house, and Raymond, you come back with a tractor."

Mr. Cole walked back to his car and stood there in the rain, looking down at the Englishman. Rumsfeld turned toward him and Stevens quickly leaned back and rolled the rear window down. Mr. Cole started explaining to the Englishman what was going to happen and never even noticed Jesse Potts coming up behind him. He finished talking and Stevens was about to roll the window back up, when Jesse leaned past Mr. Cole, stuck his head in the open window, and cleared his throat.

"'Scuse me, Mr. Rumstein," he said in his raspy voice. "You got anything to drink?"

The Englishman slowly turned his face back to the front.

Now, what Mr. Cole said to Jesse, I'll leave to your imagination, but the good news was, it suddenly stopped raining. Then the sun came out and lit up the cotton fields. I walked to the front of the car and stood looking up at the sparkling sky and the dark cloud bank moving away to the east. Turning back, I saw the Englishman staring at me in that same way again. As I started by, the Englishman nodded, and this time he rolled the window down himself.

"Good morning, young man."

At first, I was too startled to speak, but then I stammered, "Good morning, sir."

"Mr. Beatty has explained the problem to me and how he intends to remedy it. Most inconvenient, I must say, but I suppose it was unavoidable."

"Oh, yessir," I replied. "Mr. Cole wouldn've had this happen for the world. We'll be back with a tractor before you know it."

Mr. Rumsfeld smiled and said, "I was wondering if you would remain behind with me and Stevens."

I glanced to my left and saw everybody staring at me with puzzled looks on their faces. "Why, yes sir," I replied, "if it's okay with my daddy."

"Why don't you ask him then?"

"Daddy," I called, "Is it all right if I stay with Mr. Rumsfeld till you get back?"

My daddy frowned, but said, "I reckon so."

"Now ask Mr. Beatty to come up."

"Mr. Cole," I called, feeling really foolish, "Mr. Rumsfeld wants to see you."

The boss lumbered up with the mud drying on him and bent down toward the car window.

"Mr. Beatty," said the Englishman, "I'd like very much

if you went back with your men so that I might rely on a prompt return. Would you do that for me?"

"Why yeah, uh, yessir. And you say you want Little Ray to stay with you?"

"Yes, I think it might be nice to talk to him. By the way," he added. "I have been most favorably impressed with your fields."

Mr. Cole regained that grin and winked at me before walking back to his men. I watched the truck back away, turn around at a wide place in the road, and head toward the house. Then the car door clicked open and I turned to see Stevens beckoning me into the Packard's front seat.

I climbed in and turned toward our visitor. Mr. Rumsfeld smiled again and said, "Tell me, my boy, does everyone call you 'Little Ray?'"

"Well, nossir," I said, "just the folks on the farm. That's also my daddy's name. I mean Raymond's my daddy's name."

"Ah," said the visitor, forming a steeple with his fingers. "Then does anyone call you Junior?"

"No, sir," I replied, "and I hope they never do."

The Englishman's smile widened, then faded, and he sat quietly for a long time, gazing out over the fields. Finally, he said, "I had a son."

I could hear Stevens suck in his breath as the Englishman continued: "My son's name was Charles."

I was afraid to say a word because I had studied enough English to understand what "past tense" meant. That's how Mr. Rumsfeld was speaking about his son. Charles Rumsfeld was no longer living. All three of us sat there for the longest time without saying a word. I couldn't stand it any longer, so I blurted out, "Did something happen to him?" The Englishman kept staring out the window, but Stevens was looking daggers at me. Finally, the Englishman said, "I'm afraid so."

I figured I'd already said too much and I wasn't about to say anything else. Besides, Stevens looked like he wanted to throw me out of the car.

"How old are you, Little Ray?"

"I'm ten years old, sir."

"Ahh, just so, just so," said the Englishman. "I thought as much. He was the same age."

We all sat silently, but Mr. Rumsfeld kept looking at my face and glancing away again. To break the spell, I smiled and said:

"I know Mr. Cole appreciated what you said to him, sir. He was hoping you'd like what you saw."

The Englishman stirred himself and said, "Oh, yes, yes indeed. I've never seen finer crops. Your Mr. Cole needn't worry about that." I heard a soft chuckle. "He certainly got himself covered with this Delta mud, didn't he?"

I had to grin when I remembered how Mr. Cole had looked, especially when his tail end hit the ground. I looked at the Englishman and we both busted out laughing, the Englishman slapping his leg at the same time.

"And poor Stevens," he said, "who, I'm afraid, still hasn't the foggiest notion what 'give'er the gun' means."

Stevens turned to look at his Master, a sheepish look on his face.

"Well, Mr. Rumsfeld," I declared, "that might be so, but he sure didn't have any trouble figuring out what 'go, Stevens, go' meant."

"Oh, my goodness no," said the Englishman, laughing

again. "And tell me, my boy, whatever possessed his man to approach me, asking for a drink."

"I don't know, sir," I replied, "but I thought Mr. Cole would die."

"Well, I'm glad to hear that Mr. Beatty has some conception of proper propriety." Seeing my vacant look, he leaned forward, patted me on the shoulder, and said, "Never mind." Then settling back in the car seat, Mr. Rumsfeld went back to being what Mr. Cole had called a "reserved" Englishman. He got real quiet and I knew the chitchat was over. Finally, he heaved himself forward and said, "Well, in spite of the mud, I believe I'll take a walk in this delightful sunshine. You may remain with Stevens, Little Ray." With that, he opened the back door, climbed out, and commenced walking down the road, looking right and left at the cotton fields.

Stevens watched him for a minute. Then he turned to me and said, "That's the first time I've heard him laugh in a very long time."

I gave the servant a quick glance and noticed he was observing me the same way as his boss.

"It's remarkable," he said.

"What's remarkable?"

"Why your resemblance to young Charles. You could almost pass for his twin."

"What happened to him, Mr. Stevens?"

The valet placed both hand on the steering wheel and closed his eyes for a long moment. Then he said, "Very well, I shall tell you the story:

One morning, about a year ago, Mr. Rumsfeld finally relented to his son's repeated pleadings and took him to their textile mill in Manchester. He had refused up to then, because he felt the mills were too hazardous for a small child. However, the one in Manchester was not currently in operation and therefore deemed safe. There had been a temporary shortage of cotton, but a shipment was due in that very day."

We both looked toward Mr. Rumsfeld. He was still standing there, staring up at the sky.

I had to swallow before I asked, "What happened at the mill?"

"Oh, the boy was killed in an accident, sir, a most freakish accident, and not within the plant at all."

I was still watching Mr. Rumsfeld. He was standing in the middle of the road, but now he was looking back toward the car. Suddenly, I realized I didn't want to hear any more of this story. I'd already heard enough. But Stevens's strained voice kept on going. It seemed like he didn't want to tell the rest of it any more than I wanted to hear it, but now that he'd started, he had to get it out.

"The boy and his father had gone out to the loading dock to watch a truck discharge its cargo. The driver had already swung open the rear doors and was backing toward the dock. Charles caught a glimpse of the cotton bales within the truck and ran forward to get a closer look. His father shouted 'STOP' and the boy tried to obey, but he'd reached a patch of grease on the dock and he just kept sliding forward. He came up to the edge and teetered there for a moment, his little arms flailing the air. Then, his momentum carried him over. The driver never saw him or heard anything. The rear end of the truck caught the boy and ground him back into the dockside and..."

Stevens's gaze was fixed on the windshield, but I knew

he wasn't looking at his boss. He was seeing the whole thing again.

I said, "You were there, weren't you, Mr. Stevens? You saw it all."

After a pause, Stevens said, "Yes, I was there, and I've wished a thousand times that God had placed me someplace else. Had he done so, I would never have heard the screams."

In a dead voice, I heard myself say, "Charles's screams."

"His one scream, sir. The others came from the father. And those are the screams I keep hearing in my nightmares."

Out of the silence came the pop-popping sound of a John Deere tractor. My daddy was driving it, and Mr. Cole, wearing a clean shirt and pants, was perched on the tow bar behind him. I got out and watched the tractor approach, mud flying from the big rear tires. My daddy stopped behind the car, hooked a chain to the bumper, and made short work of backing the Packard out of the low place. By that time, Mr. Rumsfeld had returned to the car and Mr. Cole was behind the wheel again. I climbed up on the tow bar and my daddy pulled into the field. Mr. Cole backed passed us, turned around on a nearby crossroad, and headed for home. The Englishman was sitting in the rear seat. He never turned his head.

My daddy looked over his shoulder and grinned at me. "I thought you'd be riding back with your new friend."

"Nossir," I said, "I think we've finished talking."

My daddy gave me a funny look, but didn't say anything else. We headed back up the road.

They were all waiting for us when we got back to Mr. Cole's house. Mr. Cole and the Englishman were sitting at a little round table on the porch, drinking a cup of coffee. Stevens was standing on the steps with Mr. Rumfeld's bag in his hand. Mr. Cole was saying, "I'm sorry we didn't have no tea, but I hope the coffee will do."

"It's fine, Mr. Beatty. Please convey my compliments to Mrs. Beatty, and thank her for providing a place to freshen up. And now," he said, getting to his feet, "I believe we have a train to catch."

I was standing on the steps with Stevens when he came down them. Mr. Rumsfeld stopped and slowly turned his head. "Would you render me a service, Little Ray?"

"Yessir," I replied, "just tell me what to do."

"Take very good care of yourself," he said.

I don't think anybody heard him say it but Stevens.

The Packard pulled out of the yard with Mr. Cole driving. He kept looking over his shoulder at the Englishman and talking a mile a minute. Mr. Rumsfeld and Stevens sat still as stone.

Our house is located down the road a ways from Mr. Cole's place. It's not real big, but it's big enough for the three of us and it's tight against the weather. Also, it's got a tin roof, which I like, because of the sound the rain makes on it. Looks like I'll get to hear that sound tonight because the thunder keeps rumbling outside and I think it's getting closer. It's almost midnight and my mama and daddy have gone to sleep. I'm usually asleep myself by now, but I keep tossing in my bed, thinking about Mr. Rumsfeld and Stevens and poor little Charles. I can still see the Englishman in the distance, staring back down the road while Stevens tells me his story.

And then, another thought comes to me, and it's so sudden and clear that I sit straight up in bed. The Englishman *knew* what was happening in the car and that was why he'd gone up the road in the first place. He expected his valet to tell me about the son. There was no way he could say the words himself, so he wanted Stevens to tell me about Charlie. I don't understand why he wanted that, but I hope it made him feel better.

It's starting to rain again. I go to the window and stand there, listening to it hit the tin roof, and watching swaying curtains of it, lit by lightning and moving across the cotton fields. It's moving east, headed toward the Atlantic and maybe toward some distant shore. I can't help wondering if, after a time, this same rain will come to England and begin to fall on Mr. Rumsfeld's grand house and his two textile mills and on little Charlie's grave. And if it does, I hope it becomes a special kind of rain, one that washes away the bad memories and waters the good ones. Then, maybe Mr. Rumsfeld and Stevens can rest easier in their minds.

The Legend of Shaker Mose

Shaker Mose belonged to Lucius Johnson. He didn't really, of course, even though "Loosh" Johnson was the biggest landholder on and around Crowley's Ridge. This was the year 1923, modern times, and black men no longer belonged to rich landowners. But Shaker Mose said he did, and then he always added that, of course, Loosh Johnson belonged to him, too. "Him and his whole family. Dey all do."

Think about that for a moment. Here was Loosh Johnson, old, stern, feared by just about everybody, undisputed patriarch to that vast clan of Johnsons and all who married Johnsons and all the offspring from that. Rich, powerful, and a law unto himself, this very same Lucius Johnson belonged to a short, chunky, black man who lived alone in a log cabin on Loosh's place and appeared to own nothing but the clothes on his back.

But Shaker Mose said Loosh Johnson belonged to him and no one disputed him. Loosh Johnson never did and it's a pretty sure thing that somebody, at one time or another, went quivering and quaking to the old man and told him what Shaker had said. Shaker Mose wouldn't have cared one way or the other. He had been with Loosh all his life and, even though he no longer did any real work, he was as much a part of the Johnson world as the land itself.

Shaker Mose was two hundred years old. He told everybody he was two hundred years old and said it with all the solemnity that could be projected from a five foot, four inch body, clothed in an old faded pair of overalls and a beat up felt hat. Mose's face was as black as coal smoke and surrounded by a short, well trimmed gray beard. He seldom smiled and his expression was always one of enormous gravity.

"Cose I'm two hundred years old," he would say. "I seen two wars, ain't I, and don't de Bible say dey'll be a war evuh one hundred years."

So much for that.

Shaker Mose was walking down a dirt road one day and came upon a group of the Johnson children being taken to school by Birdie Wise, old man Loosh's housekeeper.

"Hidy, Uncle Mose," they all chimed in with grins on their faces.

"Hello, chirren," Mose gravely greeted them. "Mornin' Birdie Wise," he said to the old black woman.

"Where you goin', Mose?" asked one of the younger girls.

"Goin' to help Miss Ida Johnson plant her garden, chile."

Ida Johnson, an elderly spinster and Loosh's aunt, had passed away the week before. Shaker obviously didn't know about it, but Birdie brought him up to date.

"No you ain't, Mose," she said with a kind of terrible finality.

"I *know* I am," said Mose. "I do it evuh year."

"Well, it's time to skip it," said Birdie. "Miss Ida's dead and buried and Reverend Sam Johnson done preached her funeral."

With this, the children shrieked with laughter, despite the subject matter, while Mose, with no change of expression on the solemn face, stared for a moment at Birdie Wise. Then, he squared his shoulders, and with dignity intact, turned and headed back up the road from whence he came. The children stared after the small retreating figure and their laughter turned to smiles. They sure loved Shaker Mose.

Everybody told Shaker Mose stories. Once, Loosh took Shaker into town, and while they were in Oglesby's Grocery, one of the local rednecks began the inevitable teasing.

"How come you never got married, Mose? Must be some little darkie will have you."

"Wuz married once," Mose told him. "She passed but I ain't forgot her. Had de prettiest hair. It was long and silky and hung most to her waist."

While the redneck turned purple at this obvious description of a white woman's hair, and Loosh Johnson gazed thoughtfully into the distance, Shaker, with a reminiscent expression on his face, walked slowly out the door.

Carl Claggert was Loosh Johnson's foreman and he felt no fondness for Shaker Mose. Shortly after Loosh hired him, he actually tried to put Mose to work, and of course, that idea died aborning. Mose gravely informed Claggert that he no longer worked, had stopped back in 1903, as a matter of fact. He thought it was on a Tuesday. Since old man Loosh seemed to acquiesce in the matter, Claggert forgot about it and decided to avoid Mose. However, Lucius would occasionally tell Mose to ride with Carl as he made his rounds (Carl thought it was for some sort of fiendish pleasure the old man got out of it) and off they'd go in the dusty Model A truck, Carl driving and Mose sitting in dignified silence beside him.

They returned from such a trip one day and Mose walked down to his cabin while Carl went inside the Johnson house to report to the old man.

Loosh was sitting in front of the fireplace, cleaning a shotgun. "Well," he inquired, "did you see Dee Potter?"

"Yessir, I seen him," said Carl with that self-important air that was habitual with him. "Caint say he was glad to see me, though. Especially after I got done talking to him."

"What did you say?" asked the old man.

"Well, sir, just what you told me to, told Potter he was a sharecropper on your place. That meant he could live on and use your land, but half of everything he grew belonged to you. I told him that load of corn he sent over wasn't near 'bout half and you knew it. Told him I knew it, too, and he could damn well send over at least another wagon load or he'd have *me* to deal with."

"I'm surprised you didn't have a fight on your hands," said Loosh in a bemused tone. "Old Dee can be a tough customer."

"Oh, he started toward me like he wanted one, but I told him if he desired to get his butt kicked over a load of corn, to come on. It was all right with me."

"Where wuz I at?" came a querulous voice from the open doorway.

"Well, then he started to back down," said Carl, trying to ignore the small, dark figure behind him. "Said he wasn't thinking 'bout no fight."

"Where wuz I at?" Louder and more insistent now, the voice could scarcely be dismissed. However, Carl made one last, valiant effort.

"I said, 'Potter, the only thing you need to do is get that corn over to...'"

"WHERE WUZ I AT?"

Carl could take no more. He whirled to face his tormentor, yelling, "I don't know where the hell you was, old nigger."

"Well, ah tell you where I wuz, *Mistuh* Carl Claggert. I wuz in my place, right there beside you, and de most you said wuz—and here Mose's voice rose to a high, plaintive, quavering whine—*'Well, Dee, I sho hope you ain't mad at me, 'cause I know you honest. It's jist all in de old man's mind.'"*

Carl Claggert was struck utterly speechless. Emitting a small strangling sound, he brushed past Shaker Mose and lunged through the door. Once outside, his voice returned and he muttered a formal prophecy to the surrounding darkness.

"Someday," he said, "somebody's going to kill that old nigger."

Inside, Shaker Mose, unruffled and unperturbed, strolled into the kitchen to see if the cook had laid out anything for his supper. And old Lucius Johnson turned his grim countenance toward the fireplace and smiled at the burning logs.

Carl Claggert's prediction never came true. Nobody killed Shaker Mose. He lived on Lucius Johnson's farm until Loosh died and then he lived there among Lucius's family.

One gray, winter morning, he failed to emerge from his one-room cabin. Loosh's oldest son, George, forced the door open and found him in his narrow bunk. Mose was lying on his back with both hands crossed carefully over his chest, meeting Death with his usual composure.

And so passed into memory, Shaker Mose, two hundred years old and then some, symbol of the human spirit's victory over status and circumstance. He was buried on the place, and for a long time afterward, fresh flowers would be placed upon his grave. It was the children who brought them.

Glenda

"Roy, don't forget to feed the dog," Glenda said, and I noticed the worried frown. I knew she was thinking about me.

"And don't forget to feed yourself," she said.

"Honey, don't worry. The dog and I will be just fine."

"I'm not so much worried about Foxy. She's more self-sufficient than you."

"Well, tell you what. I'll just watch Foxy and do what she does."

"Good idea," she said smiling. "Well, guess I'd better get a move on if I'm going to catch that flight. See you tomorrow night." And she raised her face for a kiss.

I watched her drive away in the sporty blue Mazda and smiled at the license plate. It read GLENDA, her sole surrender to vanity. The small car rounded the top of a hill and disappeared from view.

I went back in the house and heard Foxy in the back yard. She was whining so I walked into the kitchen and looked at her through the patio doors. She stopped the noise and stared back at me, a little buff cocker spaniel with silky ears and dark, soulful eyes. She wasn't hungry or she would have been pouncing against the door glass. The glass in both doors bore the marks of past hungers and entreaties.

Glenda had bought her at a kennel one Saturday afternoon and surprised me by knocking on the door and then placing Foxy in my arms. The little dog had begun squirming around and licking my face. Then, Glenda was wriggling up against me and licking my ear and we all tumbled into a laughing heap on the floor. Glenda had already named her, said she was going to call her Foxy because she was just . . . *"Foxy."*

Out in the hallway, I walked toward the rear of our house and into my study. There, the typewriter and blank sheets of paper waited like an ancient debt. I wasn't in the mood but knew that sometimes, if I forced myself to start writing, the mood would change.

Our bedroom was on the left and I went in to get my reading glasses. They lay on a headboard above the bed, along with a small volume of poems by William Blake. The book belonged to Glenda, who happily recited poetry to me at a moments notice.

I looked around the bedroom and Glenda was everywhere. She'd picked out all the furnishings and decided on the colors, but I knew that many of her selections were made with me in mind. She knew I hated cramped rooms, and although this one was fairly large, she'd put mirrors in strategic places to give a feeling of space. The green tinted wallpaper was in Glenda's favorite color, but the wallpaper was there because she knew I preferred it to painted sheet rock.

And the two paintings were purchased just for me. They were reproductions of Van Gogh's "rain" landscapes and they hung, dark and somber, on the farthest wall. I stared at them and remembered her laughing comment.

"Rain paintings," she'd said. "Lots of people like Van Gogh and they usually like his sunflowers or the irises, but not you. No, *you* like the ones with crows flying in the rain."

Then she had gone out and gotten them.

I thought of Glenda in this room, how she would stand with her feet close together in front of the dresser mirror and stroke her dark hair with a long-handled brush and laugh at something I would do or say and murmur:

"I can't believe you did that," or "I can't believe you said that."

And how we made love in our huge bed.

Today, tonight, and the next day. Tomorrow seemed a long way off.

I walked into the study and sat down before my typewriter. And the silence of the house overwhelmed me. I tried to pick up where I'd left off, the story had been going fine, but now the few lines I typed seemed stilted and awkward. And in that stillness, the clacking of the keys sounded like skeletal fingers, tapping in a tomb.

I got up from the typewriter, knowing it was no use, and went into the den, into greater silence. My gaze fell on the television set and I walked over and switched it on. An announcer's welcome voice filled the room and the screen slowly came to life.

The words, *Special Report,* appeared and I slumped into

an easy chair to watch. The next picture showed a line of cars on the expressway. None of them were moving. At the front of the line, a huge cloud of smoke was billowing up near a sign reading: AIRPORT ENTRANCE. The TV camera zoomed in at the base of the smoke and the cause of it all became very clear. A small car had rammed into the side of a tanker truck. The truck sat crossways on the highway and the car was engulfed in flames. I couldn't see the car very clearly because of all the fire and smoke, but I could see that it was blue, and I could read the license plate. I sat very still with no thoughts at all in my head and I don't know how long I remained in that chair, looking at the screen.

After a while, the front doorbell began to ring. It rang and rang, but I didn't get up. Someone had come to tell me what I needed to know, but I didn't get up.

The doorbell rang and rang.

The Golf Match

Sam Boling pulled a quarter from his pocket and held it in his fingers. He placed a thumb under the edge and flipped the coin skyward. It spun above them, reflecting quick glints from the afternoon sun.

"Heads!" proclaimed Barbara.

The quarter landed and she leaned forward. A metal eagle met her scowl, its wings uplifted as if to ward off a blow.

"Damn, just once I'd like to start off with the honors."

"A sign of things to come," said Sam.

He lifted his three wood from the bag and strolled to the first tee on the nine hole Overton Park Golf Course. The fairway stretched wide and straight before him. He placed his ball on the wooden peg and stood over it, waggling his club back and forth. Taking a quick backward turn, he swung forcefully and smashed the ball into flight. A loud grunt blended with the crack of impact. The golf ball sailed down the fairway, then began its inevitable turn to the right, arcing further and further in a long, banana shaped flight. Sam sighed and turned to his wife.

"My usual slice," he murmured.

"Well, that's one of your qualities, dear. You've always been consistent."

Barbara smiled as she passed him to tee up her ball. She never used the lady's tee when playing with her husband. They were both evenly matched. Sam hit the ball further but his slice subtracted from the distance. Barbara's balls flew straight no matter what club she used and this was one of life's great mysteries to her partners, especially after they learned that she had never taken a lesson or read an instruction book..

Sam watched his wife pause over the ball and felt a momentary pang at how lovely she looked. A short, pleated skirt hanging above slim legs, a blue midshipmen's blouse, and the flowing dark hair, all contrived to make her look younger than her forty-nine years. She brought the club head back slowly and hit into the ball with a smooth, unhurried swing. It leapt into the air and soared straight as a string above the grassy fairway. Barbara stood with legs apart, watching it go, and marking where it came to rest near the fairway's center.

"Nice shot," said Sam and walked over to their pull carts.

"Thanks," she answered, following him. "We've both got good shots to the green."

They started down the fairway, pulling the two-wheeled carts behind them. A breeze swept across them and moved into the nearby forest. They could hear the fluttering and the rustling of the leaves.

The cover and bed sheets rustled softly as Sam drew them under his chin. He felt cold. Barbara lay with her back to him and Sam knew that she was not asleep. He knew that her eyes were open.

"Impotent," the doctor had said. That was the word he finally used after Sam had pressed him to use it. "You'll always be that way," he'd said. It was a physical collapsing, not psychological, and it had pillaged him very suddenly. No pill or mechanical device could help him. The doctor recommended that he tell his wife right away. Sam had not told her right away. He'd needed all the failures after his doctor's announcement and the same verdict from other doctors before he came to do it. He had told her in bed tonight. His wife had lain for long moments before finally whispering, "Thank you for telling me." She'd said nothing more and they both lay silent in the darkness.

Sam stood away from Barbara while she completed a full, graceful swing. He followed the ball's flight and saw it land on the green, bouncing once and rolling within ten feet of the pin. He walked over to his ball. Aiming left to compensate for his slice, he lofted his ball into the air and watched with satisfaction as it turned toward the center. It passed over the pin and finished on the far edge of the green. He two putted for a par and so did Barbara. They finished with an even score.

The next hole was short, a hundred yard par three. Sam again took the ball out to the left and again watched it arc to the right, sailing over the green and landing in rough grass. He ruefully watched as Barbara's shot dropped next to the pin and lay winking at him in the sun.

"My slice is God's special curse on me," he said, before thinking of the other.

"I think you're trying too hard," she replied. Before thinking of the other, she added, "Every problem you have starts with that."

Sam had drawn one of his presents from beneath the tree and turned it over in his hands. He unwrapped it and saw that it was a golf club, a special kind. He remembered seeing it in a TV ad. Barbara had probably seen it too. The club's shaft was designed so that if you swung too hard it would break down in the middle. However, if you swung in the approved smooth manner, it would perform just like an ordinary club. Sam held it out by the grip and smiled his thanks at Barbara. And at that moment, the shaft gave way in the middle and club head dropped limply toward the floor. There was a moment before the implication dawned on them. Then Barbara giggled and Sam was forced to laugh along with her. He even decided to tell her an old joke that had sprung unbidden to his mind when the doctor revealed his news.

It seemed another doctor had confronted an old country boy with the same diagnosis by saying, "Willie, I guess you know that you're impotent." And the patient had responded, "Wal, if you say so, Doc, but I ain't nearly as imPOtent as you are." There were questions in his mind but he dared not give them voice. He was afraid he'd see the answers on her face. "Does my inadequacy anger you or do you just pity me? Will you find yourself a lover? And can you tell me what will happen to us now?"

"How are you going to play that?" she asked, eyeing the half hidden ball.

"Just watch," he replied.

The golf ball nestled deep in the grass, but Sam tapped

the back edge and it hopped up, landed on the green, and trickled toward the pin. Sam watched with elation then dejection as it stopped a foot short. Barbara tapped in, and he, after a long pause with his putter, did the same. She had him by a stroke. They played even through four more holes. On the sixth tee Barbara hit her usual straight one, and Sam, lining up toward the left, lashed his ball toward that side of the fairway. It flew along the tree line before turning more and more to the right. But his allowance was accurate and the ball came to rest just in front of the green. He finished in three more strokes and Barbara used four. The score stood even again.

They smiled at each other and walked off the green. Their love of golf was a constant with them and they had played together for years. The sun sank lower and rested above a bank of shadowy clouds. The day darkened.

Sam pulled into his driveway and switched off the headlights. Barbara had forgotten to turn the porch lights on. He walked in darkness to the front door, opened it, and went inside. His wife was not in the living room nor the kitchen. He called her name.

"Back here," she answered.

He walked down the hallway and entered the bedroom. Barbara was busy screwing a light bulb into their bedside lamp. She finished, flipped a switch, and the bed lay bathed in blue light. The light reflected on the room's flat surfaces and made them gleam. It passed over the hollows and crevices leaving dark depths. Barbara turned to him and smiled, her teeth shining in the strange glow.

"What's all this?" he asked.

"Something different," she replied. "Do you think it's too kinky?"

"Barbara, this won't help anything."

His wife gazed at him, her face a marble mask, and Sam wondered if she had been thinking of him when she bought the blue bulb.

They came to the ninth and final fairway, which stretched back toward the clubhouse. The sun had grown large and bronze and was passing behind the dusky cloud bank. Barbara leaned over the ball and her shadow stretched down the fairway. Sam sat on a stone bench, watching the scanty skirt fluttering around her thighs. She waggled her club and prepared to swing.

A car had turned in from a side street. It came down the drive and rolled slowly to a stop beside the fairway. Barbara looked up and the man driving the car nodded his head. She glanced back at Sam, then stared at the ball for a long moment. Sam watched her take an awkward swing. The club head glanced off the top of the ball and it dribbled forward and came to rest a few yards from the tee. Barbara walked over to her cart and silently waited.

Sam positioned his ball and stood over it. The driver felt immensely heavy in his hands. He raised it without thinking, and swung, not caring about where the shot would go, not really caring about anything at all.

A sharp click sounded and his golf ball rose above the shadows, speeding down the fairway, gaining height, soaring straight and true toward the distant green. On and on it sailed and higher and higher it rose and it never turned and finally it vanished in the fading sunlight.

Sam gazed into the space where his ball had been and a feeling of pride and pleasure rose in him, washing like clear water through his deadness and dread, and leaving, just for a moment, the shining recollection of that wonderful shot, the best shot of his life.

He turned back to his wife. Her gaze was fixed on the car. It pulled away and both watched it move into the distance. He walked over to where her ball lay and she followed after. Without looking at her he said, "Do you want to go on, Barbara? I mean, do you want to continue?"

"After what you just saw?" she asked.

"Yes," said Sam, speaking very softly. "After all, it's only a golf match."

"Yes," she murmured, "that's all."

Barbara hit her second shot (Sam didn't really watch it) and they headed down the fairway, their golf carts trailing behind them.

And the cloud bank finally swallowed up the sun and darkness descended and the two retreating figures grew very hard to see.

Storm Creek Lake

I drive along the gravel road and watch trees move past our open windows. Their dusty leaves hang motionless in the sun. My wife, Cora, turns toward the back seat and says, "Sorry about the AC, folks. It hasn't worked for a week. The repair shop has us on their waiting list."

The couple in the back seat give her an understanding smile. "It's okay," the man replies, "there's a nice breeze back here." Neither have spoken much since the journey began. At first, I attribute this to the heat, but now I know it's because of a shared taciturnity. The man is tall, thin and angular, his knees jutting upward from the floorboard. The wife sits comfortably, her back curved, one hand resting lightly on the car seat. Her speech and all her movements are slow, languid. Cora has informed me that the man is in charge of several convenience stores. She has even given me an unasked for description of his duties. About the woman, she has little to say.

A small boy sits between them, looking straight ahead, hands clasped in his lap, the shoulders rounded forward. His features are formed by Down's Syndrome, an extreme case. The epicanthic fold is very prominent on either side of the nose. Since starting out, he has occasionally startled us by making a high-pitched, grunting sound. It comes from deep within his little throat and is his substitute for words.

"Are we getting close to the lake?" Cora asks me.

"Yes, it's at the bottom of the next hill."

The car picks up speed on the descending road and I place both hands on the steering wheel. The loose gravel causes the rear end to slightly fishtail.

"You should see the gate soon. The doctor says it's on the left."

I nod my head. Cora works for a doctor and he has told her we could use his lakeside cabin for the weekend. The couple in back were in his office at the time seeking treatment for the boy, whom they call Buck. Like many Down's victims, he suffers from heart problems. Cora knew them from repeated visits, and with the doctor's permission, invited them to come along. "It'll be good for the boy," she'd said.

Maybe for us, too, I thought. Once, not long ago, Cora laughingly told an acquaintance, in my presence, that "we used to be lovers, but now we're just good friends." Her comment has stayed in my mind.

I notice the woman watching me in the rear view mirror and I must think for a moment before I recall her name.

"Ever been out this way before, Marcy?"

"Once, a long time ago," she finally replies. "My father took me fishing on the lake." She continues to regard me through the mirror.

We reach the top of the next hill and the gravel road winds downward. After a moment, I see the lake's surface glinting through the trees.

The gate bars a narrow dirt road, which disappears into the forest. It's made of iron, half covered with rust and fungus, and secured by a large padlock. We pull up before it and Cora hands me the doctor's key.

The cabin, a structure of weathered cypress, stands among some oak trees by the lake. Their leafy branches reach over it and the sun shining through them casts dancing patterns on the roof. The man, whose name is Carl, stands by the car and stretches his arms above his head, looking around in his placid way.

We gather our belongings and climb the steps to a high porch. Cora fetches another key from her handbag and unlocks the front door. The boy runs past us through the doorway and we follow him inside.

Green light filters through the windows, which are small and covered with cloth curtains. More light is needed. I go around and pull the curtains aside.

"Look at that!" exclaims Marcy.

She faces a large black and white photo, hanging on the wall. In it, two couples stand and stare solemnly back at her. The men wear severe black suits with string ties and the women have on full length, puffed-sleeve dresses. Behind them stands a general store. You can see a churn displayed in one of the windows. Marcy steps closer to the picture. She seems absorbed in it.

I look about the room, surrounded by dark oak paneling. On the far wall, a shotgun rests on a shelf. A box of shells and a hunting knife lie beside it. The wooden floor is bare and furnishings are sparse. A table with four chairs sits next to the kitchen nook, and across the room there's a stuffed sofa and a recliner. A pot bellied, wood burning stove occupies the center.

Cora walks across the room and inspects two open doorways. "Well, which bedroom do you folks want?" she asks. "The one on the left is larger."

Marcy strolls past me and squeezes my arm. "We'll take the left one, if that's OK."

Cora nods and we carry our bags into the other bedroom. The walls are covered in the same oak paneling. On the wall in front of me, another black and white photo hangs in a plain wooden frame. It's the face of a woman and she stares back at me with dark and thoughtful eyes. She is one of the women in the living room picture.

We all walk down to the lake and stand on a wooden pier. A metal johnboat boat floats in the water and is secured by a nylon cord. It bobs gently with the waves.

"Anyone game for a boat ride?" asks my wife. "I saw an outboard motor under the porch."

"The boy wouldn't do it," says Marcy. "Look at him."

The child has not followed us onto the pier. I turn to see him standing a few yards up the hill, both hands clenched into fists. The small face is vacant but his eyes are wide with fear.

Later, we sit at the oak table and finish the ham sandwiches my wife has brought. Cora is in the kitchen alcove getting coffee when the wall phone beside her rings. She picks it up, listens for a moment, and beckons to Carl. I can hear him mumbling but can't make out the words. He returns to the table and sits heavily.

"I have to go back into town tomorrow, trouble at one of the stores. Listen, do you mind if I borrow your car? I should be back by noon."

"No," I reply. "Take as long as you like. Shame you have to go, though."

"Well, that's convenience stores for you. It's a nickel and dime business full of nickel and dime people."

I look up surprised. His placidity has been broken. He has said a clever thing. I am more surprised by Cora, by her instant, hearty laughter.

Much later, I awaken to the sound of wind gusting through the oak trees. The window air conditioner hums above my head, but the wind is louder. A limb scrapes across the cabin roof.

"Be still, Buck." Marcy's voice reaches me through the bedroom wall. Lightning turns the window pane into a strobe. A flickering glare fills the room. For a moment, the woman in the picture is illuminated. Her eyes are deep and fathomless wells. Darkness returns and the thunder finally crashes and rain lashes against the cabin.

"Uuuhhnnneee!" A whining groan, rising above the storm. "Be quiet, Buck," the woman softly responds. "Be still."

* * *

Carl places his son in the front seat and climbs in beside him. I bend over so that my face is even with his.

"You sure you can't leave him with us? He'll get used to things eventually." There is no conviction is my voice.

"No," he says. "I can tell. He'll be afraid all the time. He'll be a lot happier with his grandmother."

Carl pulls out of the yard and the rear wheels spin briefly on the rain soaked grass. He turns to wave. The small figure beside him stares through the windshield. I have come out to see them off. The two women are still asleep and I remain outside so as not to disturb them. I walk down to the water's edge and then return to the cabin.

The little outboard lies just under the porch. I drag the motor out, heft it onto my shoulder, and carry it down to the pier. I've just secured it to the boat when I notice an image wavering in the water. I look up to see the woman standing above me. She's wearing the same short cotton gown that she put on for bed. She's faces away from me and squints into the morning sun, a hand cupped over her eyes. The sunlight streams through the thin fabric and her body is darkly visible. She stands with legs apart and I can see the cleft of her buttocks, the outline of her slender waist. Marcy finally strolls back along the pier and steps off onto the sand. She turns to give me a long look. Then, she starts along the shoreline and is hidden by the wooden pier.

The motor requires only a couple of pulls before coughing into life. It settles down to a smooth drone. I push away from the pier and twist the throttle. The little boat leaps forward. Its bow rises and a foaming wake builds behind it.

I turn left and follow along the shoreline. She is there. I can see the white gown moving through the trees. Suddenly, she turns back toward the lake, walks to a sandbar, and stands staring out at me. I cut the motor and the boat drifts slowly toward her until its bow is scraping across the sand. She turns again and walks back to the tree line. Facing me once more, she takes both hands and lifts the gown from her body. The sun gleams through the treetops and her bare skin is dappled with the light. I step out of the boat and hasten forward, and Marcy kneels and spreads her gown upon the sand.

My return to the dock has been a slow journey through remorse. I tie the boat up and sit for a while, staring across the water. Finally, I enter the cabin and find it empty. I walk out on the porch and there is Marcy standing on the pier. She turns toward me and beckons with her fingers. I walk down to her and we exchange a long look. Marcy patiently waits for me to speak.

"She's not in the cabin."

"Maybe she went for a walk."

"Went for a walk where?" I ask

"Along the lake bank."

I feel as if something has crawled into my stomach and died.

"Hopefully, in the opposite direction," adds Marcy with an indolent smile.

"This can't happen again."

"I know," she answers, "and it won't."

We stare across the lake's rippling surface. Purple thunderclouds are building in the distance, and a sudden breeze brings the smell of rain.

"My father used to bring me out here fishing."

"I know. You already told me."

She turns toward me and the breeze blows a strand of dark hair across her face. "Don't be sorry for what happened. I wanted it and I wasn't disappointed. Were you?"

"No," I murmur, remembering.

"It's done, and it's just something I'll think back on once in a while. No problems."

"If she didn't see us."

"She didn't."

I look into her face and Marcy shakes her head. "She didn't." And I'm eased by the certainty in her voice.

She gestures toward the water and says, "My daddy told me that in the beginning there wasn't any Storm Creek Lake. There was just Storm Creek, a little stream. Then the Army Engineers put that dam across it and the whole valley filled up with water."

"Yes, that's right. Before that happened, people lived here and worked the land. There's a house and barn off to the west there, about halfway across the lake."

"How do you know so exactly?" she asks.

"Old maps. Old survey charts. I've studied them."

"Someone's house and barn. And now they're under the water."

"About a hundred feet of water."

"It's strange," she says, "to think of them still down there, still standing. You can almost imagine the people, see them down there, too."

"The people all left before the flooding began."

"Of course," she says.

I glance back toward the cabin. Still no sign of Cora. We walk back up the hill and I see my wife coming toward us, along the dirt road. She's holding a bouquet of violets. Her hair is ruffled and she's smiling.

"Where have you been?" I ask. "I was worried."

"Oh, when Carl left, I remembered he didn't have the gate key. I took it to him. He was waiting at the gate when I got there."

"Waiting at the gate? Waiting for what?"

"Well, I don't know," she says. "I don't think there was room enough to turn the car around."

"Why wouldn't they walk back?" I ask. "It isn't very far."

Cora hurries past me. "Oh, come on," she says. "Let's get some breakfast. I'm starving."

Carl returns in the late afternoon and Cora insists we take a boat ride. I sit in back with the motor and our guests find a place on the middle seat. Cora sits facing them in the bow. Carl's arm is around his wife's waist and I watch it undulate. He is massaging Marcy's breast. The little motor skims us over the surface of the lake and the boat shudders slightly in the waves. Heavy clouds still threaten in the west. Lightning glimmers through them, followed by a low rumble of thunder.

Cora peers around the couple and gives me a tight-lipped smile. "I think we might head back now," she says.

I lie in bed and read and listen to Cora clearing away the dishes. Marcy and Carl have retired to their bedroom. The reading lamp lights up the walls and my eyes are drawn to the woman in the picture. I wonder what connection she has to this cabin or the cabin's owner. Perhaps she and her companions were among the sturdy survivors on Crowley's Ridge, were here in the valley before the lake was created, and are now buried beneath its waters. There is a sense of how admirable they were.

Cora enters the bedroom without looking at me or speaking. She sheds her dressing gown, climbs into bed and lies on her back, staring at the ceiling.

Presently, from the other bedroom, comes the regular, rhythmic sound of creaking bedsprings. The sound comes faster and louder, and just before the creaking stops, I hear Marcy's grunting, nasal cry, much like the cry that came from her frightened son.

I get up, pull on my clothes, and stand staring at the woman in the picture. Finally, I turn around and walk over to the bed. Cora's gaze remains fixed on the ceiling and her eyes are filled with tears. I reach over and turn off the lamp. My wife's voice comes up from the darkness. "Where are you going?"

I find I must swallow before I can speak. "I don't know, maybe back to town."

"You mustn't take the car," she says. I go out the door without answering.

The night has grown older and the weather has cleared and the lake reflects a star-filled sky. I stand at the edge and gaze down at all the sparkling lights.

The surface roils and ripples and I begin to discern, beneath that body of water, a house and barn with equipment scattered about. And in wavy outline, I see farm animals and a family of people going about their work. A team and wagon appear on a distant hill and descend toward the farmhouse. In the wagon are two couples. The men have on dark suits with string ties and the women wear puffed-sleeve dresses. The family gathers in the front yard and watches the wagon approach. There is happy anticipation among them. They are all friends who hold each other to high standards. Adultery among these people would be atoned for by someone's thrusting knife or the blast of a shotgun. They are formidable people with no illusions and their lives are shaped by reality.

It's only a short walk from the cabin to the main road. I reach the gate, climb over it in the darkness, and start walking back to town. I'm uncertain what I'll do when I get there. By then, it will be morning.

Images, real and perceived, of what happened at the cabin and what is happening there now, seethe through my mind. A night bird flutters in the bushes and I hear the crunch of gravel beneath my feet. I have many miles to travel and I quicken my pace.

But instead of moving forward, it seems that now I'm descending into some shapeless void and traveling through an indefinable space where all that has happened and all that *will* happen is nothing more than a waking dream or part of a watery fancy, and I am one with those who dwell in Storm Creek Lake.

I hear tree frogs singing and feel the touch of a damp night wind and realize that I have come, once again, into the physical world. I am standing alone on Crowley's Ridge with wide eyes searching the darkness. And finally, within that shifting darkness, I perceive quite clearly the action I must take. All our adulteries must be atoned for in the manner of the Lake People, and that with a thrusting knife or the blast of a shotgun. Behind me in the cabin, those weapons lie to hand.

    I slowly turn around and head back the way I came.

Paddy's Peaches

The Irish came to Memphis before the Civil War, impoverished and hungry. Most of them settled in the city's northwest section and cast about for work. Other Memphians began calling this area the "Pinch Gut District" as many of its inhabitants went about with their belts and apron strings drawn tight against empty, shrunken stomachs. Eventually, the Irish gained some prosperity and a measure of padding about their middles but their neighborhood retained the same, though slightly gentrified, title. It would always be called the Pinch District.

For as long as the boy could remember, his grandmother had lived in the Pinch District comfortably ensconced in the same wooden house. And in a span of time beyond his remembrance, she had shared it with his grandfather, a man his grandmother had spoken of in only the vaguest terms. Paddy Callahan had been a "good provider" or he had been a "hard worker." The old woman's three lady friends, elderly themselves, with wrinkled countenances and wild gray hair, would thrust their faces close to the boy and mutter other things:

"A mean drunk," they whispered in dry and cracking voices, "and meanest to Jessie, the only one ever cared for 'em."

The boy, still young enough to be petted and pampered by old women, would simply nod his head and pretend he was a party to their ancient knowledge. He had never known his grandfather, knew very little *about* his grandfather. Even his widowed mother was reluctant to talk about this now mysterious figure. The women did relate two creditable things about him, which the boy took as truth. In the spring of 1865 Paddy Callahan left a field hospital near Petersburg and came home to Memphis. Here he recovered from his wounds, aided by his neighbors and honored discreetly, the Yankees being a pervasive presence in the city. The other thing was this: somewhere in the deep south, midst the smell and smoke and heat of battle, and over the endless marches under a southern sun, the old man had acquired a taste and a craving for peaches. He couldn't get enough of them, and back home and in their season, he ate of them constantly.

"Oh, laddie, you should've seen him," one of the more trenchant of the old ladies said, "shuffling along the sidewalk and munching on a ripe peach with the juice dribbling down his chin. He always wore this great, gray coat with wide side pockets bulging out from the peaches he kept stored in 'em. No wonder they started calling him *Peaches*. Oh, yes, that's what *everybody* called him, called him that to his face, though Paddy never minded. It was all the same to him, bein' drunk most of the time."

"But what happened to him," the boy would insist. "Where did he go?" And the response would be:

"Go? Why nobody knows, child. He just disappeared. Nobody's heard of him in fifteen years. Go? Why to the devil, I suppose, and good riddance, too." And all the old women would nod their heads in agreement. They also scolded him about questioning his grandmother, a person too sensitive, they said, for any evil reminders. "He beat her," proclaimed one, her face a seamed and settled mask. "Fix your mind on that, boy. He beat her, and that was like stepping on a butterfly."

"Why come in, Billy." His grandmother spoke in a soft, southern voice and with the faint Irish brogue that she'd never quite lost. "Don't just stand there in the doorway."

She rocked slowly back and forth in her straight-back chair. The boy pulled up a stool and sat at her feet.

"How do you feel today, grandma?'

"Oh, middling, I suppose. Are you keeping out of mischief?"

"Yes." A sly grin. "Well, most of the time."

"Let's go out to the back porch, Billy. I do enjoy the sunsets."

She reached for her cane and he helped her arise. They walked slowly to the back porch, the boy holding her elbow. She waited, standing frail but erect, while he went back and brought the rocker. He helped her settle into it and patted her on the shoulder. Pointing her cane toward a corner of the back yard, she murmured:

"Some of the peaches are ripe."

"Yes, ma'am," he answered, remembering that his grandmother usually called that spot the peach orchard. Why, he didn't know. There were only two trees there, growing so close together they looked like one. He watched their fluttering leaves.

She sat without moving, her soft, white hair falling to either side of an unlined face, clear blue eyes gazing across the yard, appearing delicate and frangible, looking as if the same breeze lifting the peach leaves could also waft her upwards from the chair.

"Billy," she asked. "How does it go in school?"

"Good, grandma," he answered. "I make good grades."

"I'm sure that you do," she said. "What's your favorite subjects?"

"Oh, I like English and literature, especially literature.

"Ahh! Anything else?"

"Well, I'm kind of interested in geography."

"Geography? And do ye learn about Ireland, then?"

The boy could not tell if the heavier brogue was real or feigned. He asked, "Do you miss Ireland, grandma?"

"Oh, Billy, I don't remember much about it. I was only ten years old when we crossed over. Your grandfather was quite a bit older than me. I've heard *him* tell some stories, sad ones about being hungry and no food in the house."

The boy sat quietly while the old questions rose up in his mind.

"He wasn't always the way you've heard, Billy."

Startled, he lifted his head and stared.

"I was little more than a girl when we married and your

grandfather was most protective. He was very kind and sweet-tempered. Then the war came and he went away and I didn't see him for a very long time. He came back weak and wounded. And he was different from before."

"What do you mean, grandma?"

"Oh, it was the war," she said. "It was Shiloh and Chickamauga and all the other places. To Paddy's mind, he'd been everywhere and seen everything. Now, nothing looked important."

"Was he cruel to you, grandma?" He had finally dared to ask it.

"Well," she said, "toward the last he was."

Yes, the old lady thought, toward the last, Padraig Callahan had been very cruel indeed, and his change from the good to the bad occurred in a place far removed from her ken and comprehension. As she'd told this inquisitive grandson, it was because of the great Civil War, because of what he'd seen and done in it, that had transformed a loving, caring husband into someone who loved no one nor cared about anything at all. On the night before he left, he'd brought her a basket of violets and gently laid it in her lap. The following morning, he and a group of friends, all Irish, had marched away south to join up with General Johnston. It was a morning in March with all things bright and blowing. As they passed by the house, her husband had grinned and thrown her a kiss.

Four years later, she watched a stranger limping up this same street toward her, and even after he drew near, she failed to recognize him. The left leg was wrapped in bandages where the trousers had been cut away and a scruffy beard covered his jaw. He was grasping a wooden walking stick, which he occasionally swung in front of him, as if fending off an assailant. He cursed as he swung it and she realized the man was drunk. A black felt hat, full of holes, was pulled low over his face and bloodshot eyes glared from under the brim in inpatient malevolence.

"Well, whaddaya waitin' for woman?" he'd shouted. "Caint ye see your husband needs a hand?"

And that had remained his temper, more or less, in all the years that followed.

Paddy and Jessie, sitting across the table from each other with a candle burning between them. Soft nighttime in the Pinch District and the muted sound of neighbors talking to each other over backyard fences. Paddy taking a pull from the whiskey bottle in front of him before tearing a peach apart and swallowing a mouthful in one convulsive motion. Watching her as a cat watches a mouse. The dinner she had prepared for him, lying untouched on the table.

"Well, what the devil are *you* so quiet for?"

"I didn't realize I was, dear," she'd replied.

I didn't realize I was, dear. The cruel mimicry. "Yes, but you never lack for somethin' to talk about with them three old cronies of yours, do ye? All four of you sittin' and talkin' about poor Jessie's trials and burdens, and all on account of that no good Paddy Callahan."

She lifted her chin and looked him in the eye. "I have never made a disparaging remark about my husband to anyone."

"The hell you haven't," he roared, rising from his chair. "You're like all the rest. Oh, yes, nobody in the Pinch could do enough for me when I come back from battle, but now I'm just a figure of fun, some clown called Peaches Callahan. And *you,*" shaking his fist, "you, in all them years, never spoke up for me or lifted a finger to help me."

"That's a lie."

The three words, softly spoken, but delivered with a fearless defiance, sent the blood rushing to Paddy's face. He stalked around the table and stood behind her. She waited for what was to come and was determined she would not cry out. The savage slap to the side of her head rocked her sideways, but her chin remained uplifted and she never did cry out. Her husband stared down at her a moment, then lurched out the front door. Only then did Jessie place a hand to her head and release the scalding tears.

"And then he left you."

It was her grandson's voice, edging into her consciousness, bringing her back to the present. The old lady stared at him and blinked her eyes.

"Wha—? Oh, I'm sorry, Billy. Well, I suppose I left *him* first. One night he came home very drunk and he tried to . . . Anyway, I went and spent the night with your mother. I came back next morning and he was gone, all his belongings gone too."

"And you've nothing to remember him by?"

"Nothing but the peach orchard. Those are his trees. He was so fond of peaches, you know."

The boy left her as dusk descended on Locust Street, first making sure her legs were draped in a coverlet, and that a lamp, hanging above her, was lit. She wanted to stay on the porch a while longer. He headed down the darkening street toward his mother's house. Neat frame dwellings and well-tended yards appeared on either side. The honeysuckle was in bloom, growing along the wooden fences and filling the boy's nostrils with its musky scent.

"Billy," came a voice from one of the porches.

He looked up to see Mike O'Neill standing in the shadows.

"Stop by the park on your way home," he said. "There's some friends of your grandmother wants to talk to ye."

The boy walked over to Mike's fence and asked, "Who are they, Mister O'Neill?"

"Why who else but them three old comrades of hers. The ones that appointed themselves her guardian angels. They passed by a little while ago. Said they'd be waiting in the bower."

"Do you know what they might want?"

"Nope, but you can bet it has something to do with their chum." Catching the boy's apprehensive tone, he added. "Don't worry about it, son. There's no real harm in them."

Billy nodded and continued on, a puzzled look on his face.

He approached the tiny neighborhood park with its familiar wooden gazebo. There was just enough light left to make out the three old women sitting inside it. They were all staring at him and one lifted a beckoning arm. As he walked toward them, they seemed to shimmer like ageless apparitions, or, the boy thought, like Macbeth's witches, waiting to deliver their prophecies. Drawing closer, he made out the familiar faces: Sarah and Nora and Kathleen, all surviving their long dead husbands.

"We've been waiting for ye, Billy," said Nora, showing a gap-tooth smile. "Come and take a seat with us."

The boy sat down and looked from one to the other.

"Nora leaned over and said, "We want to talk to you, Billy."

"Yes, ma'am," he said. "Talk to me about what?"

"About your infernal questions, boy," exclaimed Sarah, placing bony elbows on her knees.

"Questions?"

"Yes, questions about that old man. Can't you see how they plague your grandmother."

"No ma'am," he replied honestly. "I never thought they did."

"Well they do, and there's got to be a stop to it."

"Shush, Sarah," said Kathleen. And studying the boy, she asked, "So what do we tell him."

"Tell him the truth and be done with it," replied Sarah. "He's Jessie's grandson. Let him hear it all."

A full, ivory moon was rising through the trees, seeming enormous among the branches. Its shimmering light flooded the little park and stretched a shadow, straight and black, away from the gazebo.

"All right," said Kathleen, "but where will that leave *us*?"

"I think," said Nora, "that it will leave us relieved."

The boy watched the old women and saw a common assent.

"We thought," began Nora, "to tell you Paddy had run away with some woman. Lord knows there were enough of them. But now, you'll hear the facts."

"Fifteen years ago," murmured Kathleen, "Has it really been so long?"

The boy said, "Please, Aunt Nora, (he called all of them 'aunt', though they weren't related to him) tell me what happened."

"He came home drunk as usual," she said, "with the smell of cheap whiskey about him. We were all sitting in her parlor, drinking tea, when we heard him outside, bellowing some Irish pub song. Jessie's face just crumpled up and she pleaded with us to go."

"She was worried we'd get hurt," croaked Sarah, "and her with the arms and neck all covered with bruises, put there by that brave Peaches Callahan. She was so gentle that a wild thing would eat from her hand, and that devil..." The old woman broke off, took out a handkerchief, and roughly rubbed at her eyes.

"She kept begging us to leave so we did," continued Nora. "We were going down the porch steps when he lunged past us and slammed the door behind him. We paused in the front yard, and inside we could hear him yelling, and just barely, we heard her soft voice trying to reason with him. Then we heard her scream."

"I'll never forget it," broke in Kathleen, "the sound of that scream and the sight of her bursting through the doorway and down the steps, both arms stretched out in front of her and the hair flying behind and her eyes wide with horror. She didn't even notice us when she flew by and ran on down the street."

"Then out *he* came," said Sarah. "He'd torn off his shirt and he stood there with his bare chest heaving while he shouted curses after Jessie. He started down the steps and I saw the great iron skillet in his hand."

"We blocked his way," whispered Kathleen. "Oh, Mary Mother of God, I was so scared, but we couldn't let him get her."

"There was murder in his little pig eyes," said Sarah,

"enough murder for all of us. He swung the skillet at Nora, but he missed and it slipped from his fingers. He stumbled and fell to his knees and I snatched the skillet up and whacked him across the nose. He howled and tried to get up and I hit him again. This time, I had all my strength behind it, and when the edge of the skillet connected, I felt his skull cave in."

All the boy could do was listen. He sat frozen, incapable of movement or speech or even thought. Nora placed her fingers to his cheek and said:

"When Sarah hit Paddy the second time, I took the skillet from her. We all looked at each other, and if we'd spoken our agreement it could not have been more plain. I raised the skillet and brought it down again upon his head."

"She handed me the skillet," said Kathleen, "and I dealt my own blow to Peaches Callahan."

The boy finally found his voice and blurted, "But didn't anyone see you?"

Nora removed her fingers and said, "Billy, things were a little different back then. There were fewer people here and there weren't any street lamps. We all peered around. Nobody was in sight so we dragged him to a corner of the back yard. I went back to the front and stood watch while they took pick and shovel and dug a shallow grave."

"We were mortally afraid Jessie would come back and see us," said Kathleen, "but I figured she'd gone to her daughter's house and that's what she did. She didn't return till morning."

"For some reason," said Kathleen, "I didn't think it proper to bury him half naked, so we got his torn shirt and his old coat from the house and put them on him. I can still smell that coat. There were peaches in the pockets, overripe peaches giving out an odor."

"One in each pocket," declared Sarah, "It sort of balanced him out, you know, kept him on an even keel for his trip to purgatory."

"We went inside the house and gathered up all his clothing and his shaving gear. We placed them with him in the grave and covered everything up. We were all there when Jessie came back next morning. We had our story prepared, and to this day she's never heard anything different." Nora paused, for a moment, staring into the past. "We told her Paddy had collected his belongings and left cursing. I took both her hands in mine and said, 'Jessie, I don't think he's coming back.'"

The old women went away and the boy sat there for a long time, thoughts darting in his mind like the bats, flitting through the gazebo. He still wasn't sure why the old women had told him of their great crime, why they trusted him with their secret. He supposed it was as they said. His questions about Paddy Callahan had distressed his grandmother, troubled her more than she'd ever let him know. But *they* knew. She had divulged it to them, perhaps unwittingly, and they had once again banded together as a living shield for their lifelong friend and ward, their treasure, their *butterfly*.

So Grandfather Callahan had traveled no further than a corner of his own back yard, where he'd been planted, so to speak, along with two of his peaches. And they grew up out of his pockets.

How many times, in the following days, had his grandmother sat at her accustomed place on the back porch, wondering where Paddy had gone, wondering if he'd ever... And then, in one bright, perceptual flash, the boy realized why the old women knew they could rely upon his silence. He envisioned Jessie Callahan, rocking in her chair and gazing across her yard. Jessie Callahan, looking at a mound of new-turned earth that had not been there yesterday, eventually looking at the two trees growing from it and knowing full well from whence they sprang. She had said they were Paddy's peach trees and so they were, and also a part of Paddy.

For they grew up out of his pockets.

How wise these old women were, to know that he would eventually arrive at this the concluding answer to the last of his questions, and would, through a shared love of his grandmother, become their *second* accomplice.

The boy sighed and closed his eyes. He was recalling this afternoon and the final moments with his grandmother. She had risen, cane in hand, and asked him to walk with her to the corner of her back yard. They came up to one of the trees and she had waited while he plucked a ripe fruit from one of the lower limbs. He'd handed it to her and Jessie had balanced it for a moment in her upturned palm. Then, she had bitten into the peach and chewed on it thoughtfully, a look of quiet contentment on her face.

Mexicans

All the Pillow Farm families were talking about the Mexicans. The farm's leafy cotton plants stretched out row upon row and acre after acre and the Mexicans would soon be here to tend them. These foreign people would come up out of their foreign land and live among us for six weeks. The agriculture agent had already told us that none of them spoke English. They would have no interpreter. Everyone wondered how we would talk to each other.

And on a crystalline spring morning in that year of 1957, they came. My uncle and Morgan Mitchell and I waited beside the highway to greet them. My uncle did not look happy. He was the Farm Manager, hired by the Pillows to oversee it all: the planting, the harvesting, the maintenance, *and* the care of six families. He did not need this added responsibility. Morgan didn't look happy either.

He was the unofficial spokesman for the farm's black folk and saw himself as their leader and advocate. He viewed the Mexicans as a threat. I'm sure that I looked happy. This would be a new experience, an adventure, and any sixteen-year-old boy would thrill to that

Presently, we perceived a distant vehicle. It grew larger as we watched, took on a definite shape, and became a beat-up bus. It groaned to a stop and sat silent and motionless before us. Then the door swung open and the Mexicans came out. They came out slowly, carrying cloth bags and looking about. I counted twenty of them as they lined up beside the bus. All were slight in stature with thin, wiry builds. They had on faded work clothes, mostly jeans and denim shirts, and all of them wore hats with wide brims. They stared out from beneath them with dark and watchful eyes.

I visualized how they must see us: one dignified Caucasian, a wrinkled and frowning old black man, and a skinny boy. Picking out the boss had to be easy. One of them approached my uncle and removed his hat.

"I Diego," he announced. Turning toward the others, he said, "This workers."

My uncle, always a courteous and courtly man, nodded and extended his hand. He looked at me and I knew this was my cue. I had recently purchased a Spanish grammar book. Remembering what I'd read, I stepped forward.

"Buenos dias," I squeaked out. *"Mi nombre es,* Ramon."

I'd no sooner gotten out my name than they were clustered around me, slapping me on the back and talking away. I felt my face burning and held up both hands.

"No, no," I protested, *"No hablo mucho espanol."*

The Mexicans stopped talking, but continued to smile. My uncle motioned toward our truck and they walked to the back of it. As they passed, a few touched me on the shoulder and I grinned and forgot my embarrassment. *"Bienvenido,"* I murmured, *"bienvenido."*

Earlier, the agriculture agent had visited my uncle and explained what had to be done. "They must be furnished with adequate housing," he said. "They should have the means to prepare their meals and a table to eat from. They must have a supply of clean water and a place to bathe. Also, in case of sickness, they must be provided with medical care. And," he concluded, "you have to transport them into town each Saturday night to lay in food and supplies."

My uncle ruefully shook his head and asked, "How often do they get to sleep with my wife?"

A picture, featuring my Aunt Nora, flashed through my mind and I blushed a deep red. I did that often in those days. The agent chuckled and said, "Now John, you know the government is reimbursing all those expenses. They're even paying you for the time you spend. Just save the receipts and fill out the forms."

"Well, I hope they're worth the trouble. And I hope they're worth their pay."

"Don't worry," the agent said. "I've watched them on a few farms south of here. You'll get your money's worth."

And so it came to pass that the Mexicans were brought to their house. It wasn't much to look at, just an unpainted shack in the middle of a cotton field. But my uncle had ordered it cleaned up and screens had been installed on the windows. Cots, chairs, and a table and cook stove now sat in its four rooms. The Mexicans stared silently at their new home, then lifted their bags and went inside. Morgan watched the last one enter, heaved a great sigh, and walked away mumbling.

The agriculture agent was right about the Mexicans. On their first morning of work, I picked them up in the farm truck and transported them to our southeast section. The air was filled with the smell of new growth and the sound of Spanish as the men disembarked with cotton hoes in their hands. It was immediately apparent that they were no strangers to these hoes or to cotton fields. Each worker picked a row and all quickly worked their way down the field, arms moving rhythmically and the bright cutting edges of the hoes flashing in the sun. I left them and passed by a few hours later on some errand for my uncle. They had cleaned a large area and were going as strong as ever.

At noon, I drove by once again and the Mexicans had gathered under the shade of a sycamore tree. I could see the orange flame of a small fire and wisps of smoke drifting under the tree limbs. They all looked up, recognized me, and began to wave. I turned onto the dirt road leading to the tree. They watched me stop and get out of the truck, smiles on all their faces. One of them, clearly younger than the rest, said, *"Mi nombre es Tomas."*

"No, no," came several laughing voices. *"No es,* Tomas. *Es,* Tacho."

It took a moment for me to understand that Tacho was his nickname, probably bestowed by his fellow workers. They all began to introduce themselves.

"Mi nombre es, Antonio," said one of the darker ones, and *"Mi nombre es*, Luis," came from a taller one on his left.

"Un momento, un momento," I cried, and fished in my shirt pocket for a pad and pencil. I wrote down the names and a one or two word description. The Mexicans watched me scribble away and when I looked up I caught their

expressions of quiet approval. They continued giving their names until a final worker was left, the one who had spoken to my uncle. He stood slightly apart from the others and I suddenly realized that if they had a leader, this older one must be him. "You're Diego," I blurted.

Diego smiled and nodded his head while his companions gathered closer.

"Mi nombre es, Ramon," I told them for the second time.

"Si, Ramon," they answered, but Diego shook his head.

"El nombre del pequeno patron es, Rojo," he said and the others burst out laughing.

I reached inside the truck and pulled out the grammar book. After a moment, I blushed and looked up at Diego. He had said: "The name of the little boss is Red." The old Mexican smiled and tugged at his hair. I grinned back, realizing how peculiar my carrot-colored mop must look to these swarthy people.

"Si," I consented, *"mi nombre es,* Rojo."

I walked over to the fire and saw a tin sheet laying over it. On the sheet rested several flat pancakes, just turning brown. One of the men pulled on his gloves, lifted the sheet off, and set it beside a pot of simmering pinto beans, recently removed from the fire. He pulled off the gloves, and taking a wooden spoon, ladled some of the beans onto a pancake. He rolled the pancake around the beans and handed the morsel to me. I took a bite of the moist tortilla and chili spiced beans and found the food delicious. Rolling my eyes, I took another huge bite, and even Diego joined his companions in laughter.

The Mexicans worked the rest of the week and all of Saturday morning. That afternoon, they lined up on their front porch and my uncle paid them off. After much page turning, I informed Diego that we'd be back to take them into town.

"I was afraid they'd run out of groceries," said my uncle.

"Well," I said, "They don't eat much, mostly beans and tortillas."

"And they cook them right out in the field?"

"Yessir. Well, they cook the tortillas. They just heat up the beans."

"Did you eat some?" asked my uncle, giving me a sideways glance.

"Sure did," I replied, "tasted pretty good, too."

I was driving my Uncle John's pickup. He sat beside me and gazed out across his fields. "Do you like them, Ray?" he asked.

"Yessir, I guess so. We don't do much talking."

My uncle chuckled and let his hand rest, for a moment, on my shoulder. "I'm glad you're getting along with them," he said. "You are the Pillow Farm's ambassador to its Spanish workers."

I blushed and murmured, "Thanks a *lot*." But his little joke sent a current of pleasure through me.

We pulled into the equipment shed and sat surrounded by tractors and farm implements. I breathed in the pungent mix of fuel, grease, and fertilizer. My uncle handed me a key and said, "Go gas up the truck. You and Morgan can take them into Medford."

Although only sixteen, I had driven the five-ton Ford with its high sideboards into town several times before. Still, I thrilled at the prospect and looked forward to transporting my new friends. I only wished I could see over the dashboard a little better. With Morgan sitting at upright attention beside me, we rumbled down the dirt road toward the Mexicans' house. They were all standing in the front yard, their backs turned toward us. Something held their attention.

"What do you suppose they're doing, Morgan?" I asked

"Ain't no tellin' with them folks," he declared. "Probably fightin' amongst themselves."

I sighed and turned into the front yard. We got out and the Mexicans came to meet us. Behind them, I could see a rectangular piece of plywood, set on its end and leaning against the house. The life-size figure of a man had been sketched on it, and at the figure's left chest there appeared a crudely drawn heart. Tomas, the boy called Tacho, was trying to yank a hunting knife from the heart. He worked it back and forth a couple of times and the knife came free. Its blade and handle must have been a foot long. Tacho drew a soft, flexible scabbard from his pocket and inserted the blade into it. He was about to place scabbard and knife into a hip pocket when the clamor began. His friends all started speaking at once. A couple were making throwing motions and I heard the word, *Rojo*. Tacho shook his head and began to walk toward the truck, but Diego touched his arm and pointed to me. I was nodding my head because I'd already figured out what the Mexicans were saying. They wanted Tacho to give me a demonstration. His embarrassment was obvious, but he turned once more to face the house. His fellow workers parted, leaving a clear space between him and the figure on the plywood. The small Mexican did not return to where he'd thrown the knife before. He stood where he was, and from twenty paces away unsheathed the gleaming blade. His hand performed a neat little flip and caught the blade by its tip. Suddenly, the left foot shifted forward, the right arm blurred, and I caught a flash of sunlight on metal.

Chunnk! the heavy knife struck the plywood heart and buried itself to the handle. His companions nodded their heads and a few murmured, *"Bueno."* I just stood there with wide eyes and open mouth. Tacho glanced at me and went to get his knife. Finally, I pointed toward the truck and in my slow and painful Spanish said:

"Vayamos a la ciudad. Let us go to town."

The Mexicans nodded and headed for the Ford. Tacho was the last to climb aboard and I stood behind him, waiting to close the gate. His denim shirt hung outside his jeans and covered the rear pockets, but I could see the outline of the knife.

The asphalt highway stretched into the distance and shimmered in the heat, while the flat expanse of the Delta slid by on either side, spreading toward each horizon under a green growth of cotton plants. I concentrated on my driving. My uncle had entrusted me with this mission and I was determined he wouldn't regret it. Morgan Mitchell, sitting at my side in rigid or perhaps petrified silence, was an added inducement to do well. His confidence in my driving abilities measured close to zero.

"You sho you kin see out the windshield all right?" he murmured, staring straight ahead.

"Yes, Morgan, I'm sure," I replied.

"Cause if you caint, I'll let you set on my coat."

"No thanks. I'm fine."

Grim silence followed, punctuated only by an occasional

panicky grunt when I happened to wobble or the truck wheels hit a pothole.

We reached Medford late in the afternoon and drove down Jackson Avenue toward the business section. At the corner of Jackson and Main Street lay a small cemetery with elm trees growing along its border. I parked the truck beneath the spreading branches and turned the engine off. The Mexicans climbed down and we stood there in a cluster.

Diego stepped in front of me and handed over a slip of paper. I could make out most of the words on it: flour, coffee, canned milk, and other staples.

Diego asked, *"Donde esta la tienda?"*

He needed to find a grocery store, and I of course, must lead them.

"Let us all go to the store," I haltingly said. *"Todos vayamos a la tienda."*

"Bueno," he replied, and *"bueno"* rang out around us.

And so away we went, a gawky, red-headed kid, followed by a line of twenty Mexican laborers, and bringing up the rear, an old cotton-haired black man; all headed for Oglesby's Grocery Store, which stood on the next corner. People paused on the opposite sidewalk to stare at us. One actually pointed. I blushed right on cue.

We stopped in front of Oglesby's and I held up my arms to get their attention. My companions solemnly stared while I pulled out my Spanish book. Glancing from it to them, I repeated, in what I hoped was understandable Spanish, my uncle's instructions.

"Remember where the truck is parked," I told them, "and come back to it when you finish your business. Everybody must be back by nine o'clock."

"Nueve?" one of them asked.

"Si, nueve," I said, *"Por favor."*

Diego stepped in front of me and, in a firm voice, said, *"Usted debe estar de regreso a las nueve, entiende?"*

A few nodded and said, *"Si, nueve."* They didn't seem enthusiastic about it.

Morgan and I bought crackers, bologna, and orange soda and carried it back to the truck. There, in the lengthening shade of an elm tree, we ate our supper. Darkness finally fell and I lay on my back and watched the stars. I could hear the town sounds all around me and wondered if I'd like living here. After some thought, I decided I wouldn't.

Rolling onto my side, I asked, "Morgan, would you like living in a town?"

"No, *suh*," he said. Glancing at the cemetery, he added, "Or bein' buried in one either."

"Same here," I said, and closing my eyes, I intoned:

"Go play with the towns you have built of blocks,
The towns where you would have bound me.
I sleep in my earth like a tired fox,
And my buffalo have found me."

"What wuz that," asked Morgan?

"It's from a poem," I said.

"Who wrote it?"

"A guy named Stephen Vincent Benet."

"Hmm, well when they bury me, I want to sleep jist like that."

I rolled onto my back again and let my headrest against the soft grass. The next thing I knew, Morgan was shaking me by the shoulder.

"Better wake up, boy," he said. "You been sleepin' like ole Steve Bennett said, like some tired fox."

"What time is it," I asked, rubbing my eyes.

"It's almost nine o'clock and there ain't a sign of them Mexicans."

I got to my feet and we stood there in the darkness. An old dinged-up pickup had pulled beneath a neighboring tree. Two men sat in the cab, drinking from a bottle.

"Well," I said, "guess we'd better go look for 'em."

"I knowed they wouldn't be back when they was sposed to," Morgan grumbled. "Probly all liquored up in some honky tonk."

I admitted the possibility, but I didn't really believe it. I just couldn't imagine them that way.

We had started down the sidewalk when I detected shifting shapes in the darkness ahead. And then I heard the singing. The Mexicans were moving toward us, coming in a group, and singing a soft ballad. We stopped and watched them draw near.

I counted noses as they tossed their purchases onto the truck and prepared to climb aboard. All my companions were back and calling out their greetings.

"Caint y'all keep them damn greasers quiet," came a voice from the pickup. "All that sangin' and yappin' is about to git on my nerves."

I felt a chill run down my spine and I kept my eyes on the Mexicans. All twenty heads swung in unison toward the pickup, like a herd of deer seeking the intruder. *"Vamonos,"* I murmured to them. "Let's go."

"Yeah," the voice came back. "Git 'em out of here."

"That's whut he's tryin' to do," said Morgan. "Now leave the boy alone."

I caught his eye and motioned him to be quiet, but both doors on the pickup had already swung open and the men were getting out. The driver, fat and red-faced, stood looking at us. His friend, not so fat, but with a belly hanging over his belt buckle, walked around and joined him. They both started toward Morgan.

"What did you say, ole nigger?" yelled the red-faced one.

Morgan merely straightened his back and lifted his chin. Both men came up to him and the one with the sagging belly grabbed him by the shoulder. The other seized his elbow and they began pulling him toward their truck.

I remained where I was, struck numb with shock and fear. It was then I heard, or rather sensed, someone stepping up beside me. It was Tacho, his impassive face turned toward the rednecks. I watched in bug-eyed astonishment as he drew the knife from his hip pocket and slowly pulled off the scabbard. The knife, with what seemed like a life of its own, flipped upward and turned over. It came back down and now the tip of its blade rested between Tacho's fingers. Out of the corner of my eye, I saw Diego running forward to stop him.

I swallowed and finally forced some sound from my throat.

"Noooooo." It came out in a tight, high scream.

Too late. The small left foot had already lifted. The right arm flashed forward, and that foot long knife with the glittering blade went blurring through the air.

* * *

Medford's electric luminance lay far behind us. The only light remaining was starlight and moonlight and the big truck's shining headlights, reaching into the darkness. With both windows down, we could hear the throb of the engine and the whooshing wind, and as we swept by a growth of woods, the chiming of a hundred tree frogs.

And we could hear the Mexicans.

They were singing, the notes floating on the air like ephemeral gossamer, swept up from their own dark and distant and mysterious land. Songs of soft sadness. Jubilant songs of joy. And these melodies merged with the rushing wind and the calling frogs and became one music, filling the night and reaching outward across the Delta.

My friend's head rested against the seat back and his eyes were closed. He was listening, and occasionally a small smile would play across his lips. I chuckled softly and he turned his weathered face around.

"What're *you* laughin' at?"

"I was just thinking about your two friends in the pickup."

"Weren't no friends of mine."

"Yeah, well I guess not, 'cause when ole Tacho's knife thunked into that tree, right under the guy's nose, they sure didn't waste any time deserting you."

"Uh-*uh*," chuckled Morgan, "they sho didn't. I thought they was gonna turn that truck over, roarin' outta there. Guess they figured the others had knives, too, and was gettin' ready to chunk'em."

We both started laughing and I said, "I can see it now, the air full of knives."

"And all headed toward *them*," Morgan said.

After a while, he added, "Good thing that Mexican missed. We could *all* be settin' in jail."

I looked over at him and said, "You really think Tacho missed?"

Morgan thought for a moment and answered, "Naw, I guess not. I seen the same thing you did, back at the house. He hit what he was aimin' at."

"He did it to help you," I said.

My friend didn't reply, but I thought I saw that white-topped head nod, ever so slightly. And then I remembered that, back there, under the elm trees, this old man had tried to help *me*.

I watched the fields of cotton sweep past, dark in their depths, and their tops drenched in moonlight. Silvery sight. Silver night. And all in concert with the constant music of the Mexicans.

"Will they be back in the fall," asked Morgan, "to help with the cotton pickin'?"

"I think so," I said. "My uncle wants them back. How do *you* feel about it?"

"Well," said Morgan, after a long silence, "if they want to come back, ain't nothin' I can do about that."

Farewell, Tennessee

On the night before he left, David and I sat down to supper at the Union Hotel. A few minutes later, Marcus Winchester, Ed Hickman, and Gus Young came in and joined us. Everybody was talking and joshing while they tossed down some of the Union's cellar-made whiskey and waited for the steaks. David, of course, had ordered his usual: half a dozen fried eggs and a pan full of bacon. He took a big swallow from his glass and said:

"Is old Black Hawk still in town?"

Black Hawk was a name the Indians gave to Adam Huntsman and Adam had just beaten David in their race for the U. S. Congress. They'd campaigned together and even roomed together during the contest. Huntsman sported a peg leg and David had made endless fun of him.

Marcus Winchester answered in his careful and cultured manner. "No, I cannot say that he is, suh. I believe the gentleman is, even now, clumping toward our Sodom on the Potomac, a place, I may say, that is suitable to his character."

Everyone was nodding and grinning at the major, who added, "not that I've ever been able to discern any."

The waiter brought in an immense platter and set it before David. He dug in, and with his mouth full of bacon and eggs, announced, "Well, if the people of Tennessee want to send old Timber Toes to Washington, they can all go to hell and I'll go to Texas."

"An appropriate sentiment," said Winchester, "reflecting a wise decision."

The steaks arrived and the rest of us fell to. David cleaned his platter, belched, and stretched both long arms over his head. I chewed on a mouthful of rare rib eye and regarded my long time companion, one that I probably wouldn't see again after tomorrow. The candle at the center of the table shed a saffron glow over his weathered features: the high-boned cheeks, the straight nose, the wide, thin-lipped mouth. And most notable, his eyes, large and gray, with a perpetual melancholy cast, remaining so even when their owner was engaged in some frolic of the moment. The copper-colored hair, parted in the middle, grew thick and straight and hung almost to his shoulders.

Dinner over, we got up, left money on the table, and walked outside. The night breeze rustled around us, stirring a damp mist and blowing part of a newspaper across Front Street. Charcoal clouds hung in somber layers, just above the rooftops, and were sent billowing, occasionally, by a sweep of wind. It was a chill wind. November had come to Memphis.

David started away with that long woodsman's stride,

not bothering to look over his shoulder, and we, of course, followed along. Nobody asked the destination. By common assent, it would be the nearest tavern. Gus Young leaned toward me and said:

"He's still got Peg Leg Huntsman on his mind."

"Some I guess, but I don't think it bothers him much. You know David. He's thinking more and more about Texas."

"Yeah, I reckon. You know, he never was too fond of bein' called Davy and Huntsman called him that all the time. He tolerated it in everybody else, but he hated Huntsman doing it."

"I know it," I said, "and old Huntsman knew it too."

Up ahead, I saw a coal oil lantern, burning dimly and creating a faint halo in the surrounding mist. It hung next to an open doorway and a sign reading: *Yancey's Tavern*. David wheeled toward it and we all followed him through. A table of rough-hewn oak sat in a corner. On the table, a single candle flickered, doing little to dispel the darkness. Another coal oil lamp hung above the bar and created the only bright spot in the room. The fat tavern owner came over and we ordered a jug and glasses.

"That'll be four dollars," he said.

"Hell, you ain't even brought it yet," said Gus. "What's the matter? Is the damn stuff so bad you think we won't pay you after we taste it?"

Yancey thrust out his stomach and said, "I don't keep no bad whiskey."

Winchester said, "I do not believe that you do, Mr. Yancey, but kindly deliver the product so that we may judge for ourselves." And tilting his chin toward him, he added, "And I'll hear no more of this nonsense about advance payment."

Yancey shuffled away, but not before nodding to the major. He also took a lingering look at David, trying to place him.

Gus was still fuming. "I oughta take my 'Bowie' to him," he said. "Fat bastard."

I watched Crockett's mouth spread in a grin and I knew he was about to go into one of his "Davy" acts, honed and preserved for the public. He scrambled to his feet, and with wide eyes glaring at Gus, hollered:

"Eeehaaah! there he sets, gents, the *or*-iginal, iron-bellied, copper-plated corpse maker from the wilds of Arkansas. Oh, the cryin' of the dyin' is music to his ears."

We all sat there laughing while he waved his arms about, head moving forward and back, long hair swinging, white teeth flashing, Davy Crockett with the bark on.

Gus got a sheepish look on his face and David sat down and said, "I really don't blame you, Gus. I hate a rude bartender, or a rude anybody for that matter."

"Rudeness is, of course, inexcusable," stated Winchester, "and impossible in a gentleman."

"Well, Major," said Gus, "there's very few gentlemen in Memphis."

Yancey brought the jug and glasses. Ed Hickman tossed him four one-dollar pieces and the fat man picked them up, all the time glaring at Gus. He glanced once more at David, then waddled back to the bar.

Marcus nodded at Gus and said, "I fear that you are correct, my friend." Then, looking at David, he said, "However, I believe our companion here is one of that select few."

Ed Hickman and Gus Young burst out laughing and

Ed sputtered, "Major, *you* are a gentleman and that's a well known fact, but I believe you are mistaken about that galoot sitting across from you."

"Nonetheless, I stand by my statement," replied Winchester, "because, you see, he fits the classic definition."

"And what definition is that?" asked David, looking closely at his friend.

"Why, suh," said the Major, "the one which states that: 'a gentleman is a person who is at home in any company.'"

I thought on what he had just said about David, recalled the journeys we had taken and the people we'd spent time with, and saw the truth in this certified gentleman's words.

Once, we'd drifted down the Obion with some tough river raftsmen. David was called upon to prove he was as tough as they were and he did just that, knocking Bully Johnson down over and over again until Bully lay on the tied-together logs, trying to get up one more time. David finally gave him his hand and pulled Johnson to his feet. Johnson, stood there grinning and admitted he'd been licked fair and square. All the raftsmen gathered around and slapped both men on the back, passing them a jug. Another time, we'd found ourselves in an Indian camp, sitting cross-legged in old Chief Lame Bear's wigwam, resting on soft panther skins while a sleet-filled wind howled outside, gathered in a circle with a dozen Chickasaw warriors, a bright, hickory-fueled fire blazing in the center. The flames pushed out waves of warmth and cast shifting shadows on the wigwam walls and flew as flickering red lights into Lame Bear's eyes.

"Crockett," the chief pronounced, impassive face pointed toward the fire, "honored enemy; we will pass a pipe among us and speak of old battles."

He pulled a long-stemmed pipe from behind him, already filled by one of his many daughters. Leaning forward, he plucked a live coal from the fire and unhurriedly dropped it into the bowl. He puffed on it, blew a thin stream of smoke out through pursed lips, and passed it to the warrior on his right. Finally, the pipe came round to David.

He blew out smoke and said, "I smoke this pipe of peace with Lame Bear and his clan brothers, worthy enemies. We met his brothers in the oak grove by the big river, and behind them sat a horseman. And my heart rose within me when I saw Lame Bear riding toward us, for then I knew that this would be a remembered fight."

And hearing these words, the old chief's eyes blazed and he thrust both arms toward the top of the wigwam, while an exultant, "Haieee!" burst from his mouth. The rest of his warriors joined in, along with me and Crockett, and with swelling throats, we drowned out the night wind with our yells. Haieee for ancient battles lost and won. Haieee for all the old remembered fights.

David served three terms in Congress, six years in all, and I rode up there twice to see him. During my second visit, we walked down Pennsylvania Avenue and I couldn't believe how famous he'd become. Books had been written about him, and across the country, actors portrayed him on the stage. As we strolled along, everyone from street urchins to moneyed moguls would come up to speak to him or take his hand. Plump businessmen called to him from their carriages. Ladies would ask him to autograph their fans. And

Old David acknowledged them all in the same unaffected way, laughing and joking, and if he sensed they expected it, tossing in one of his famous "brags." We stopped once to watch some children, splashing in a pond, and a staid, white-haired citizen limped up, leaned on his cane, and watched along with us.

Finally he turned, and with a gap-toothed grin, said, "Mr. Crockett, that sight reminds me of a tale they tell about you."

David faced him, placed both hands on his hips, and with feet set wide apart and a big smile spreading across his face said, "And what was that, sir."

And the old man, getting into the spirit of the thing, replied, "They tell it that you're the fastest swimmer in the country."

And David said, "Now *there's* an example of how a damn lie can grow and spread. There's several who can swim faster and even further than me. And a few can dive down deeper. There's probably a couple that can stay under longer. But, my friend, there ain't a man alive that can come up *dryer* than Congressman David Crockett from Tennessee." And the old gentleman blinked, then chuckled, and walked away shaking his head.

I never was with David when he was on the job and surrounded by other politicians, but one of them, a crony of Andrew Jackson, told me that he held his own and always got his ideas across. "He seemed at home among them," that worthy related, long before I heard Marcus Winchester define a gentleman.

*   *   *

The candle had burned to a nub, there in Yancey's Tavern, and the coal oil lamp was almost empty of fuel. We got up and Crockett tossed another dollar on the table. As we passed through the door, Yancey leaned over his bar and spoke:

"Mister Crockett."

David half turned and the fat man said: "I been ponderin' on who you was, and it finally come to me. That's *you,* ain't it? Davy Crockett?"

Before David could answer, Gus Young exclaimed, "Damn right that's Crockett, and you're lucky he didn't . . ."

David held up a restraining hand and said, "What can I do for you, Mr. Yancey?"

"Well sir, I tell you what you can do for me," said Yancey, reaching under the bar.

Gus's hand flew to his knife, and he had it half drawn when the barkeep straightened up, clutching a fresh jug. He held it out to David and said: "Take this for you and your friends, compliments of the house."

David took it and shook Yancey's hand. "And I voted for you, too," said the tavern owner.

"Well, Mr. Yancey," David said, "it appears your vote was wasted." Then holding up the jug, he added, "but this won't be." We all slapped Yancey on the shoulder as we went out the door.

The night had grown older and colder and its clammy mist came down on us like a sorrow-soaked shroud. The dank street, reflecting Yancey's lantern, led off into darkness, and somewhere in the fog, we heard the grinding of iron-rimmed wagon wheels against the cobblestones. A drover's muffled voice exclaimed, "Go 'long there, Sammy," and the grinding grew faint and finally faded away. We walked on northward, down the center of Front Street. Weather-beaten buildings, barely discernible, rose up on either side. Ed Hickman stopped, and swaying slightly, pointed to a plank structure, looming to our left.

He said, "Gentlemen, yon stands a friend of mine's mule barn. There's a counting table and chairs within and he won't mind if we use 'em."

"That is agreeable to me," said the major. "I do believe that Mister Yancey's tavern is the only one open tonight." Ed led the way and we all filed inside. He fumbled around, produced a lantern, and soon had it lit and casting an amber light. The lantern was placed on the table and chairs were brought forth. We all sat down and looked to the whiskey for warmth.

The jug went round and round and the talk droned on and on. David would throw in a word here and there, but he gradually grew silent and his chin sank down on his chest. He sat there with his eyes half-closed, waiting for Gus Young to finish his oft told tale of how he'd had his Bowie knife special made over in Arkansas. Finally, Gus wound down and David did something I'd never known him to do. With friends on either side, and a jug in front of him, he made his decision to leave. Getting to his feet, my old comrade offered his apologies and informed us he needed some sleep. Everybody stood up to shake hands, the Major last of all.

He gazed into David's eyes and said, "I hope that we may someday meet again."

Gus Young snorted, "Well, of course, major. We'll all meet for breakfast."

The three sat back down and I followed David outside. "I'll walk back to the Union with you."

"No, you keep on with the boys," he said. "There's a lot left in the jug, and you know, old Yancey was right. He *don't* keep no bad whiskey."

"Well, I'll see you in the morning," I said.

David nodded, turned around, and headed back down Front Street. A few swinging strides carried him into the fog. It swirled and closed behind him. I stood there for a while, just staring at where he'd been. Finally, I became aware of my companions' loud laughter and went back in to join them.

Next morning, I woke up early, but Davy Crockett had gone. The desk clerk said he'd checked out just before dawn, wanted to catch the daybreak ferry when it pushed out from Catfish Cove.

I walked down and stood on a bluff and watched the great river, washing its mile-wide current southward to New Orleans. Across the way lay Arkansas, and beyond that, a land called Texas. Most of it was undiscovered country where everything was new. Yet, there were people in it. And I felt that, in their company, my friend would find his home.

The Ridge and The Town

Wayne Johnson lay in bed and watched dust motes float through morning sunbeams. After a full night's sleep, he still felt tired. Also, his muscles ached, and no wonder. The last two days, normally his days off, had been spent moving his parents from Crowley's Ridge into Medford. Their furniture was old and solid. And *heavy,* he remembered, sitting up and rubbing a shoulder. He swung his feet onto the floor and sighed. This afternoon, his regular job awaited him, but first a final trip into Crowley's Ridge to pick up his mother and father. They'd spent their last night there in an empty house. This morning they must be present to sell off the last of the chickens, or so the old man said. His son suspected they were simply postponing that final departure. They'd lived there forty years and he and his two older sisters were born there. The sisters had married and left, glad to be gone, and he'd later followed them for a town apartment and a casino job. Now the property had all been sold: house and barn, livestock and equipment. Also, fifty acres of land with its hills and hollows, forest and ploughed earth. The buyers didn't pay top dollar and didn't need to. The old man and woman were only the latest in a continuing migration into town. The Ridge, once full of families, had grown empty and silent; speech and laughter gone to birdsong and a louder murmuring of the wind.

Wayne drove for half an hour before he saw the gravel road, winding up a hill on the right. He turned his old pickup off the blacktop, crunched across the rocks, and ascended through a leafy cavern of trees. The road leveled off, quit the forest, and cut through a cultivated field. He saw the house ahead, an enduring structure of stone and weathered timber. His parents stood on the front porch with a suitcase and a sleeping bag at their feet. No chickens or chicken buyers were in sight.

The ride back into town passed mostly in silence. His mother sat in the middle and the old man stared out the window. Once he turned and said:

"Did you get the electricity turned on?"

"Sure did," the son replied, "plus the gas and water."

"You had to get the *water* turned on?"

"Yessir, gotta pay for that too." He did not tell his father that he'd had to put up deposits. He felt the old man's gaze.

"Wayne, your mama and I do appreciate you helping with all this," he said in a rough voice. "Kind of messed up your days off, didn't it?"

"Aw, I don't mind, Pop. I didn't have anything to do."
"Got to go back in this evening, don't you?"
"Yep"
"Not much rest," his father commented.
"Well, I'm a security officer, daddy. All I do is walk around the casino floor and tell folks where the toilet is. It ain't like chopping cotton." The old man chuckled and his mother patted him on the leg.

The drab house, sheathed in aluminum siding, sat on a treeless lot, just off the downtown area. All three stared at it for a moment before getting out of the truck. They entered the front door and Wayne's mother walked into the kitchen. He and his father stood in the living room, talking in low voices.

"She hated to leave," said the son. *And so did you*, he thought.

"Didn't have no choice. With her heart, she's got to be near a hospital." Peering at his son, the old man said, "We'll be all right. Hell, city livin' ain't gonna kill us."

They both spoke in a tired, matter of fact tone. It had all been said before.

"Well, I gotta get to work," sighed Wayne. "I'll be by tomorrow and take you to the store."

"No need for that," said his father. "It's less'n a quarter of a mile. I'll walk it. I'll be walkin' it later, anyway."

"Naw, I'll come by tomorrow," said the young man, and headed for the door. "Call it blocks, Pop," he said over his shoulder.

"Huh!"

"It's four *blocks* to the store," he said, grinning.

"Didn't I just say that," replied the old man, and closed the door behind him.

Wayne drove down Dover Street, Medford's main thoroughfare, and remembered first seeing it as a child. His father had brought him into town on a Saturday night, both emerging out of the dark stillness of Crowley's Ridge and onto Dover Street's electric brightness and the clamor of cars and people. Much later, he and his teenage companions had prowled up and down the street in their beat up jalopies, making U turns at either end, forever circling in a rite called "Dragging Dover." Now, the Drag remained quiet on a Saturday night and pretty much deserted every other night. Its once busy stores had regressed to quiet shops, many struggling to survive. The only place reflecting bygone prosperity was Barney's Dollar Store. Tomorrow, his father, a farmer all his life, would report there for work.

The rising sun lit up his parent's house, revealing a need for paint. Wayne stood on the front porch and hesitated for a moment. He couldn't decide whether or not he should knock. Finally, he pushed the door open. His father sat on the couch, holding a paper bag. Wayne realized it was his lunch.

"Better start locking your door," the boy said, "just to be on the safe side."

"Yep, I imagine there's some things I'll have to do different."

"Well, not a lot, Pop. It's just a small town, but it *ain't* Crowley's Ridge."

"You ready to go, son?" asked the old man, rising from the couch.

"Yeah, if you are. Mama still asleep?"

"Yep, or just pretending. But she's trying to rest like the doctor said."

"Say, Pop, you asked me to speak to Barney and I did. But I still don't see why you're in such a hurry to go to work at a damn dollar store. You've got money. The farm brought in enough for you and mama to live on and your insurance will pay most of her doctor bills."

"We have to buy another truck. Remember, I sold the old clunker."

"You got more than enough for that, too."

"I need to work, Wayne," said the old man, giving him a somber smile. "You know that."

"Well, you ain't gonna like it," said the son.

Barney's Dollar Store stood on the north end of Dover Street, its burnt orange awning visible from blocks away. Wayne knocked on the front door glass. His father stood slightly behind him. Barney Cohen, the owner, came to the door, grinned out at them, and unlocked it.

"Hello, Wayne," he said, and looked over the young man's shoulder. "So this is your father." He stretched out his hand and said, "I'm Barney Cohen."

"Pleased to meet you," said the old man, stepping forward. "My name's Dosh Johnson."

"Dosh! An unusual name; don't believe I've ever heard that one."

"No, It ain't too common, I guess."

Wayne watched the two men shake hands, the storeowner short, portly, and sleek, the farmer tall and gaunt. Dosh held the soft hand as if it were an egg.

"Well, Dosh," said Cohen, taking a rearward step and holding the door open, "let's go to the back and I'll get you started." He glanced at the son, hesitating in the doorway. "Come with us, if you want to, Wayne."

They all stood in the storeroom amid towering rows of cardboard boxes. The storeowner indicated four of them, lined up by a counter. "You can begin here, Dosh. Empty these boxes and separate all the items. You know, all the girls dresses will go together, all the socks and, uh . . . whatever. Of course, if there's like two kinds of socks, *they'll* have to be separated and, well, you get the idea. When everything is sorted out, call Harold over." He indicated a scrawny youngster, staring at them from a corner. "He'll show you how to read an invoice and check it off."

Dosh walked to the crates, knelt, and began peeling away the sealing tape. "No, do this," said Barney, picking up a box cutter and kneeling beside Dosh. He made four deft cutting motions on one of the boxes and lifted the top off.

"Why, that was right neat," said the father.

"Quicker too," said Cohen with a grin.

Harold gave out a snicker. Wayne fixed him with a look and took a step forward.

His father's soft voice came from behind him. "Son, ain't you got some things to do before work?"

Wayne turned and said, "I reckon so."

The store owner walked him to the door. "Don't worry about your father, Wayne. I hired him because you said he was a hard worker. One look at him and I knew it was the truth."

"Yeah, how's that?" came the quick reply

"Hard physical work, year after year. It leaves its mark on a man," said Barney. "My father had that look."

"Well, this kind's pretty new to him."

"I know it is. Tell me, Wayne. Can he . . .? I mean, is he able to read?"

The son felt quick rancor rise. He looked sharply at the storeowner, but saw only a mild anxiety on his face. Wayne had once worked a few weeks for Cohen, and now he remembered the warmth, the gentle wit, and the kindness. They'd discovered a common interest in science fiction and were constantly swapping paperbacks. He remembered, also, that Barney was willing to hire his father, sight unseen.

"He reads well enough," he said. "He might have some trouble with that invoice." As an afterthought, he added, "He might have some trouble with Harold, too."

"Harold's a moron," answered Cohen. "Your father can handle him."

"I imagine he can. Anyway, Barney, thanks for doing this. I hope everything works out."

Barney chuckled. "Oh, it'll work out fine for *me*," he said. "Dosh will probably make the best receiving clerk I've ever had, but--"

"But what?" Wayne asked.

"Oh, I just wonder how he'll—"

"How he'll what?"

"Listen, remember the last swap we did?" said Cohen. "I gave you something called *Dangerous Planet*. Remember what you gave me?"

"Yeah, a book out of my Heinlein collection. By the way, I want it back."

"And the title?

Wayne remembered the title very well. "*Stranger In A Strange Land,"* he said. "Yes," came the soft reply. "Yes, I thought that was the one."

* * *

Wayne turned left off Biscoe Street, passed through the city limits, and approached the towering bridge. He crossed over the river, left the bridge behind, and entered another state. Eight years before, Mississippi had voted to legalize gambling and one of the results appeared on his left. The casino complex stood like some loony shopping center, all flashing lights and riotous loops of glowing neon. The river flowed behind it, and across the river lay the hazy ascent of Crowley's Ridge.

He parked in the employee's lot, entered a side door, and walked to the dressing room. There, he put on his uniform and went into the security office for the daily briefing. Twelve other uniforms stood in a semi-circle before a man in a business suit. The Shift Manager read a few bulletins and finished with the usual admonition to stay alert and not forget that they were all representatives of the El Dorado Casino. Wayne walked onto the gambling floor beside a huge black officer called Mookie. They chatted, for a moment, and Mookie lumbered to the front entrance, his assignment for the first two hours. There, he would greet customers, check IDs—minors were constantly trying to sneak into this, the mother of all arcades—and answer questions. Where the big man stood was called a "hard post" and you couldn't move from it. After two hours he would be relieved and become a "rover." That meant you roamed at will throughout the casino.

Wayne started his initial two hours as a rover. At first, his brain registered every fragment of the casino's raucous din. The slot machines rang, beeped, and buzzed, the "stick men" at the crap tables kept up a steady chatter, and a repeated inquiry of "Cocktails?" came from the walking waitresses. His two-way radio, the speaker secured to his shoulder, filled his left ear with instructions and acknowledgments, and the other ear took in the shouts and murmurs of a dozen conversations and exclamations. Then, after five or ten minutes, all of it lessened and blended into background clatter. Wayne kept attuned to the radio traffic, but the rest was muted Muzak. One thing he never got used to and could not dismiss were the clouds of cigarette and cigar smoke. He was not a smoker and his eyes watered constantly.

The first four hours passed quietly. He escorted the big money players (High Rollers) to their cars and delivered chips to the gaming tables. Once, he broke up a scuffle between two drunks, who wound up hugging and apologizing. Drinks at the El Dorado came without charge, a flood of free alcohol, and he never understood how things remained so peaceful. Over in Medford, along Honky Tonk Row, this practice would have caused a nightly killing.

At mealtime, Wayne filled his tray in the canteen and sat at one of the long Formica tables. He glanced to his right and saw Hamilton Cox munching on a cheeseburger. The old man held his sandwich in both hands and the small head, mounted on a lean, corded neck, snaked toward it when he took a bite. Cox's thin, rounded shoulders and the darting head gave him the appearance of some large, tree-dwelling bird. Hamilton dealt blackjack, and at his station he looked the same, flipping out the cards with shoulders hunched, narrow neck stretching and retracting, a vulture in the gaming pit. He, like Wayne, lived in Medford, and his parents, in an earlier year, had also come down from Crowley's Ridge.

"How's it going, Ham," asked Wayne.

"Not too bad, Wayno. Arthritis is acting up a little."

"Still just in the shoulder?"

"Yep," said Cox. "If it moves to the hands and fingers, I'm out of a job."

He pivoted toward the young man. "You get your mama and daddy into town?"

"Uh-huh, finished moving yesterday. The old man went to work this morning."

Ham's thrusting head stopped short of the sandwich. "Went to work where?" he asked.

"Over at Barney Cohen's."

Cox laid the cheeseburger back on its plate and said, "Dosh Johnson went to work at the Dollar Store?"

"Yep, in the receiving room."

"What the hell for?" asked Hamilton. "I know he's got money laid by."

"Who are we talking about, Ham? It's Dosh. You think he's gonna sit around the house?"

"No," said Cox, "I caint picture that. But then I never pictured him living in town either. 'Course, I know about Emma's health. He had no choice about moving, but he's damn sure got a choice about working in that store."

"I know," Wayne said, "and he chose to work."

"Well, he ain't gonna like it," declared Cox.

"My words exactly," said Wayne.

At midnight Wayne Johnson punched out, shed the uniform, and donned his jeans and sweatshirt. The dusty Chevy pickup waited in the parking lot. He pulled onto Highway 49 and headed toward the bridge. Crossing high above the river, he could almost feel the wash of its mile-wide current. A towboat churned beneath, headed upstream and pushing an acre of barges. The lights of Medford glimmered off to his right, ending where the Ridge loomed like a dark cloud bank. He descended toward the Arkansas shore, exited the bridge, and approached the center of town. There, he turned onto Dover. It stretched northward, narrowing into the distance. On either side, a line of streetlights shone, but the Drag lay quiet and deserted. Wayne headed down it, listening to the throb of his truck motor. Then he saw the solitary figure on the sidewalk.

The man stood in front of a pawnshop, both hands thrust into his pockets, silent and unmoving. He stared in the window for awhile, before moving on to the next shop. The contents of Hal's Toy Store could not have interested him, but he gave that display equal time. His hands now dangled at his sides. He slowly walked to the next window, then on to the next.

Wayne applied the brakes, brought his face closer to the windshield, and stared at this midnight watcher of windows, a familiar figure, yet seeming more remote than a single distant star. The young man carefully pulled his pickup to the curb, switched off the headlights, and placed both hands on the steering wheel. He watched his father walk across the street, looking neither left nor right, and paying no attention to the truck and its driver. Dosh halted on the opposite sidewalk, and for a long moment stood looking northward into the rising shadows of Crowley's Ridge. Then, he shuffled forward, rounded a corner, and disappeared.

His son started the engine and drove on down the Drag. He forgot to switch on his headlights, but it didn't really matter. The streetlights were sufficient, and even through a film of tears, he saw everything well enough. He passed the point where his father had stood and the tears welled up again. Wayne angrily brushed them aside. Damn that casino smoke, he thought. Damn it all to hell.

Charlie and Janet

Their elevator stopped in the basement parking lot of the Memphis Civic Auditorium. The doors hissed open and Charlie and Janet walked out. Charlie was thinking about the concert and his wife had to speak twice before he heard her.

"Charlie," she repeated, "unlock the car door."

They joined a line of cars and finally reached the exit. Charlie turned left on Front Street and headed south between the brick buildings. Heavy clouds moved just above the rooftops. A damp wind whipped the awning in front of a darkened restaurant and blew a forgotten menu from off an outside table. Janet looked out her window and watched the empty shops slide past.

They'd married just after Charlie joined the Price-Simpson Advertising Agency, and in the beginning they had struggled. Most of his income was based on commissions and commissions had been small. Two years went by before Charlie could make the necessary contacts and garner the larger accounts. In the meantime, Janet went to work, selling cosmetics at Penney's. They both wanted children, so when bigger paychecks appeared, they threw away the birth control pills and waited for Janet to get pregnant. She never did.

Charlie kept putting it off, but he finally went to a doctor and had him run some tests. The doctor called him back in a few days. Charlie learned that he was sterile and always would be. He never got around to telling Janet.

Charlie made more money and moved up. Janet couldn't see the need for working, so she quit. She kept house for her husband, spent time with her parents, and worked on her sewing. Sometimes Janet did needlepoint in front of the bedroom window and hummed softly to herself. She liked being by herself. She welcomed it. Her only other diversion had been a week-long shopping trip to New York and she had gone alone.

The Cadillac sped down the freeway, its headlights picking out streaks of rain. Charlie flicked on the wipers and hummed a bit of the Ninth Symphony to himself. He was trying to like classical music, trying other things as well. He was working to get his body into shape. He had thoughts of becoming a writer. Last night, he'd met his secretary for a drink.

Charlie realized, with a start, that their driveway was just ahead. He pulled into it as the rain beat down harder. It drummed on their car roof and swept across the yard in solemn sheets. Charlie moved to turn the switch off, but Janet stayed him with her hand.

"Charlie," she said. "I've got some news for you."
"Good news?" he asked.

"I think so. I'm pregnant, Charlie. We're going to have a baby."

Charlie kept staring out the windshield until Janet nudged him and said, "Well?"

He turned to her, eyes still wide and staring. Finally, he gave his wife a thin smile and said, "I'm happy for you, Janet."

"Happy for us," his wife corrected. "Happy for *us*."

"Of course," Charlie replied. "You know that's what I meant."

He finally cut the engine and the wipers stopped. Water streamed down the windshield. The porch lights shone through it and cast liquid shadows on the couple inside. They both sat motionless, and for a moment, they seemed covered in tears.

LITTLE MYSTERIES

"Crime, like virtue, has its degrees."
—Racine

Abigail and the Horse

Harry "The Horse" Belsen parked his rented Chevy on the north side of Peabody Lane and sat for a long time, looking at the house. It lay far back from the street, fronted by a rolling landscape of manicured lawn and wisteria vines. A winding driveway, bordered by magnolias, led up to a columned entrance. The whole place looked like something out of Gone With The Wind. The Horse nodded his head in satisfaction.

He enjoyed a reputation in the underworld that few burglars achieve. Among the criminal class, it's usually bank robbers and other violent characters that gain notoriety. The second story men remain an unknown or disdained bunch. But this particular burglar was just too good to be ignored.

The Houston Museum people have reason to remember a visit from Harry. Their "Kunming Cup", a Ming vase of inestimable value, now rests in the den of a Los Angeles land developer. Also, pricey antiques, fabulous jewelry and irreplaceable art have changed owners because of Harry's efforts. He once carried twelve oil paintings, still in their frames, out the studio window of an art dealer and down fourteen flights of fire escape to a waiting van. When news of that little caper reached his associates, they began to call him The Horse.

Belsen had come to Memphis a month ago and checked into an obscure motel. Through methods perfected over a long career, he quickly ascertained who the wealthiest citizens were and where they dwelled, because he'd determined before coming here that this was going to be a residential job. However, Harry, being the pro he was, took his search past the point of where the rich folks lived. He was looking for those known in Memphis as "old money," cultured people who'd had their wealth forever and liked to remain close to at least a part of it. Often as not, these members were elderly themselves, alone inside their huge houses. Abigail Wingate, resident of the mansion before him, was such a case.

Harry had acquired the necessary preliminary information about her from his highly refined resources. Although very rich, she seemed to have an aversion to banks and paid cash for most purchases. She possessed a collection of paintings and rare books. Harry figured she must spend a lot of time looking at the paintings and reading the books because she seldom went out. He also figured old Abby kept a lot of cash in her house.

Belsen decided two weeks ago that the Wingate mansion would be the target and he had monitored it ever since. Abigail employed a gardener and two house servants, but none were residents and they didn't show up on weekends.

Their employer also left each Saturday morning for some unknown destination, and returned around noon, picked up and brought back by a limo driver. Last weekend, Harry had been tempted to follow her but decided to stay focused on the house. It was enough to know that Abigail was regular in her habits. For two Saturday's running and for two long hours each time, the house had stood empty. This morning was the third Saturday. If the old lady left as usual, the Horse would go in.

Abigail Wingate sat by a front window and waited for her transportation. She always looked forward to Saturday mornings. Doctor Winston offered the most excellent tea and companionship. At precisely 10 o'clock, the limousine, sent by the doctor and charged to Abigail, pulled up in the driveway. The driver whisked her to Winston's downtown office and she swept in to receive his usual gracious greeting. Doctor Winston was one of Memphis's most eminent psychiatrists and Ms. Wingate was more than a little delusional. He'd seen her for years and they'd grown quite fond of each other. Early on, the good doctor discovered that his patient was harmless, and though her delusions appeared to be permanent, she handled them adequately and was able to function well enough in everyday society. She was cognizant of everything about her, but in her hazy view, the old world and the new existed at one and the same time. The bustling streets of modern Memphis and the sedate, carriage crowded avenues of an ante bellum city were equally real for her. And Abigail Wingate looked upon herself as a southern belle of long ago, a vision not far removed from her actual childhood, which had been one of gentility and soft politeness and the seclusion afforded by southern wealth.

Now she was quite old and Doctor Winston held no illusions about treatment. His function, he realized, was simply to monitor her actions and look after her physical well being. Truth be told, he looked forward to these Saturday visits, and being a southerner himself, the role that he would play.

"Miss Wingate," he exclaimed, coming from his office and crossing the reception room with arms outspread. "Great honor, ma'am."

"Very kind of you to invite me to your home, suh," she replied, fluttering a floral fan and extending a small wrinkled hand. "I so look forward to our conversations."

"The pleasure is entirely mine, *deah* lady," Winston murmured, getting into the spirit of the thing. "Shall we adjourn to the parlor"?

Harry, the Horse, watched the dark limo disappear in the distance before driving to the rear of the mansion. Getting through the back door was short work for a man of his capabilities, and in moments he was inside and standing in the dining hall. Belsen knew right away he'd hit pay dirt. Oil paintings hung on the walls, recognized instantly for their value, and he glimpsed other objects d'art in the hall. This was going to be the mother of all paydays. A stairway lay to his left and he sped up two steps at a time. As soon as his head cleared the landing, Harry saw the safe. It sat just in front of him, one of those old fashioned ones with a large dial and long handle, and Belsen with his professional eye noted something he couldn't quite believe. The handle was in the *down* position. This old safe was unlocked. He pulled the heavy door open and peered in at what appeared to be all the money in the world. The upstairs hallway was unlit and without windows and he saw only oblong outlines in the safe's dark interior, but Harry knew what they were. Giving a sharp cry, he snatched a plastic bag from his pocket and, looking wildly about him, shoveled the greenbacks in. They'd been neatly stacked and bound and they made a satisfying weight when he hefted the bag. All thoughts of paintings and other valuables flew from Harry's mind. He wanted only to get out, to get away with this incredible find. He plunged back down the stairs and out the rear door.

    Half an hour later, Belsen entered his hotel room and locked the door behind him. He upended the plastic bag and watched the bundles of bills cascade onto the bed. Harry picked one up, ripped off the binder, and pressed the money to his lips. A pungent, musty smell entered his nostrils and Belsen held a bill up to the light and examined it. The first thing he noticed was the picture. This piece of currency did not portray a likeness of Franklin, or Hamilton, or even George Washington. Instead, Jefferson Davis's eyes held him in an indifferent gaze, and underneath this visage, the words: "Confederate States of America" burned into his brain. The Horse's jaw dropped and his face grew pale and slack. Then, he raised his eyes to the ceiling and let out a feeble groan. There'd been a fortune in artwork back there and he'd abandoned it all for this Dixie funny money. He couldn't go back, of course. There wasn't enough time and everything was blown.

Well, there was *one* thing to be grateful for. He had worked alone, as always, and nobody, but nobody, would ever learn what had happened here today. The Horse looked down at the bed, remembered how he'd raced wild-eyed from Abigail's house, and felt his lips twitching in a smile. Then, he fell face forward across the bundles of worthless paper, slapped his palms against the mattress, and gave himself up to loud and prolonged laughter.

Black-Eyed Peas

Charlotte and Henry sat at a corner booth in Alfred's Cafe. Charlotte fixed Henry in a malevolent stare. "Let's face a few facts, Henry. You're thirty two years old, you're out of a job, you're broke, and..."

No, don't say it, he thought.

"And you live with your *grandmother*," she said.

"Haven't you forgotten two things?"

"No, Henry, I haven't forgotten that your grandmother is rich, and you're her only relative."

"And she's also very old," he said.

Slowly and distinctly, as if talking to a child, Charlotte said, "She's seventy five, my love. In our age of health care, preventive medicines, and wholesome life styles, the old biddy could live to be a hundred. By then, I'll be . . . Oh, never mind."

Henry leaned across the table and placed his hand over hers. "She might not live through the day."

Charlotte gave him a weary look and said, "Don't start again, Henry. Not with your hair-brained schemes. Once, you were gonna shove granny down the stairs, remember that? Then you decided to strangle her and make it look like a burglary. Then you . . ."

"This time it's going to happen."

"And why is this time different?" she asked

So Henry brought his face closer and told her about Leon Speers.

He'd first met Speers while sitting on a city park bench. They got to talking and Leon told him about his varied past. Seems he'd once been a pharmacist, but lost that job because of shady practices. Leon then went slightly left of the law and wound up serving two years in prison. "I imagine I'll keep on hustling," he'd said. "With my record, any legitimate employer would treat me like poison."

"Yes," responded Henry as his mind began to race. "Can you get me some?"

"Some what?"

"Poison."

"Well, yeah, I guess so. I still know certain suppliers."

Henry gazed at Speers and reflected that this man knew *nothing* about him, not even his name. He plunged ahead. "I need something that's odorless and tasteless and fatal when swallowed. And here's the most important thing. It has to be undetectable. I mean it absolutely *must* not show up during an autopsy.

Leon stared at his companion with growing comprehension. "Are you serious?"

"I certainly am."

"Well, there's a barbiturate derivative that—"

"Never mind the technical stuff. Can you get it?"

"Yeah, I can get it. Can you get a thousand dollars?"

Henry assured him that he could and knew that somehow he would. After all, it was a very small investment against such a huge return.

He left Charlotte in the restaurant and made a stop at Leon's apartment. An hour later, he was walking up the driveway of his grandmother's stately house. Henry patted his shirt pocket and felt the package of white powder. He recalled Leon's parting words.

"It's quick acting," the ex-pharmacist had said, "and painless. Whoever takes it will feel a quick chill. Then they'll pass into a deep sleep. Shortly after that, their heart will stop."

"And it won't be detected?"

"Nope. The medical examiner will think it was a heart attack."

Henry opened the front door and walked inside. He was greeted by his grandmother, who gave him a quick hug. "Come into the kitchen, honey. There's something I want you to try."

She was her usual cheerful and energetic self. Henry glanced at the petite, gray-haired figure and felt a brief twinge of conscience. Then he thought about her mountain of money and the feeling passed.

A pot bubbled on the stove and Henry sniffed appreciatively. Something smelled good. His grandmother took two glazed earthen bowls from the cabinet and ladled them full. She brought the bowls over, and with a proud flourish, set them out on the table. The old lady took a seat and beamed at her grandson.

"They're black-eyed peas," she exclaimed, "and they

came from my very own pea patch. Go ahead, Henry. Taste them."

He gave her a rueful stare and asked, "Won't I need a spoon first?"

"My goodness. Where *has* my mind gone?" She jumped up and started for a cabinet drawer.

Henry's brain was racing. This might be his only chance. "Hey, grandma, since this is a special occasion, let's use the good silverware." He knew the sterling was kept in an upright cupboard, standing in the hallway.

"Oh, Henry, you're such a romantic," she cried, and hurried out of the kitchen. Quickly, her grandson leaned across the table and emptied the powder into her bowl. He stirred it with his finger and it dissolved instantly in the soupy mixture. After a moment, his grandmother returned, bearing a spoon in either hand.

At that moment, the phone in the parlor rang.

"I'll get it," he said, and left his place at the table. He lifted the receiver and murmured a greeting.

A familiar voice said, "Hello, Henry?"

"Charlotte? What the devil are you calling me here for?"

"I just couldn't stand it, Henry. What's going on? Did you do it?"

Henry glanced behind him and lowered his voice. "Yes, but nothing's happened yet."

"You mean she's still...?"

"Yes, Charlotte, yes. She's still alive. Now get off the phone."

"Okay," said Charlotte, "but call me when it's over."

Henry waited a moment to allow his nerves to settle. Then he returned to the kitchen and took his place at the table. He raised his spoon and said:

"Here's to black-eyed peas."

"Home grown," the old lady added.

"Indeed."

He took a huge mouthful, and noticed his grandmother was already chewing contentedly. "Mmmm, these are good," he said. "I was afraid they'd get cold."

"Me too, so I popped them in the microwave. I didn't know how long you'd be on the phone."

Henry had actually swallowed another spoonful before the awful implication sank in. He stared across the table and croaked, "You put them in the microwave?"

"Why yes, dear."

"So is this the same bowl I . . .?"

Henry never got to finish his question, nor did he need to. Already he perceived the terrible chill, sweeping through his body. And he felt so very sleepy.

The Last Day of February

Lloyd and Tammy Diggens sat in their Ford station wagon and eyed the small-town bank, lying before them like an unopened present. Lloyd and Tammy had never secured an account there, but they planned on making a large withdrawal. Robbing banks was their trade. Tammy maintained that it was a growing business and they were growing with it.

Tammy was short, plump, and blond, with a quick mind and great powers of observation. Lloyd was tall, lean, and dark. His black eyes could also observe, but Tammy knew his limitations. Lloyd might be observing a bank one minute and a flock of sparrows the next. And when it came to making plans, he usually confined himself to thinking about what he was going to have for lunch. Still, he was rock solid on the job, calm and nerveless

"Well, whaddaya think?" she asked her husband.

"It looks good, Tammy. You know how to pick'em."

Tammy gave a nod of her head. It's a good layout inside, too. You'll see three tellers on the left and the manager's office straight ahead. And when I cased the place last week, I didn't see any security guard."

"Well, you know how to pick'em," Lloyd said again.

"They'll open in a few minutes," she continued. "As soon as they do, we'll go in. Pretty much the usual routine. We'll show our guns and I'll start hollerin'. You'll stay out on the floor. I'll go in behind the tellers and sweep up the cash. When I'm finished, we'll stroll out together and boogie back to Memphis."

"Tammy?" Lloyd's voice held a worried tone. "This car ran rough all the way down here. Think we should leave the motor running while we're inside?"

"Lloyd, honey," Tammy said, "we could do that. And while we're at it, we could also put up a sign saying: *Bank Robbery In Progress*."

"Well, it sure ran rough," Lloyd said.

"Tammy?"

"Yes, Lloyd."

"Where we gonna park?"

"Now *that's* a good question," Tammy said. "Did you notice that deserted house behind us. It can't be seen from the bank."

Tammy turned to see if the temporary tag was still taped to the rear window. Lloyd had lifted it from a dealership in Memphis, after removing the Ford's original plates. The tag showed *Temporary* at the top, a bunch of numbers in the middle, and a place to write the expiration date at the bottom.

"Baby, did you write in a date at the bottom of that tag?" she asked.

"Uh-huh," Lloyd said. "I wrote in the last day of the month."

"Okay, this is the sixteenth. That'll work."

Just then a young woman appeared inside the bank door. She unlocked it and walked away.

Tammy turned to Lloyd. "You ready?"

"I'm ready," said Lloyd

She turned the key in the ignition and the Ford started quickly, which reassured Lloyd. They crossed the street and backed in beside the empty house. Tammy reached under the seat and pulled out the plastic bag that held their disguises. She put on a wig and a pair of sunglasses, while Lloyd donned the other pair of shades and a cap. Tammy folded the empty bag and put it in the left pocket of her pants. In her right, she could feel the weight of the gun. Lloyd jammed a hand into his jacket pocket and clutched his revolver.

"Let's go," Tammy said.

As they entered the bank, she glanced at the manager's office. Nobody home. Three tellers sat behind their cages, waiting for the first customer. It was perfect.

Lloyd walked to the center of the lobby and was pulling the gun from his jacket when Tammy yelled, "You people get your hands up."

The three women's hands shot toward the ceiling. Tammy slammed through the swinging doors and began working quickly. When the last drawer was empty, she came back out and faced the tellers. "Don't anybody stick their nose out that door after we leave. If you do, we'll shoot it off."

She stuffed the sack of money inside her baggy pants, and she and Lloyd walked out. They strode to the station wagon and jumped in. As Tammy pulled into the street, she drew the bag from her pants and she and Lloyd placed their pistols and disguises inside. Tammy was careful to stay within the speed limit, and when a traffic light turned red, she stopped.

"Was you looking behind us when we pulled out, baby?" she asked Lloyd.

"Yep," said Lloyd. "Didn't nobody come out."

"Good," she said, and glanced in the rearview mirror. Suddenly, her stomach felt like two, huge hands were squeezing it. A police car was almost touching their bumper.

"Lloyd," she said, staring straight ahead. "Don't turn around. The cops are right behind us."

The light turned green and, as Tammy pulled away, she looked in the mirror again. The cruiser held two policemen. The one on the right leaned over and said something to the driver.

"Are they still behind us?" Lloyd asked.

"Yeah, but don't worry," she said. "They're probably on the way to a donut shop." Then she said something else, but Lloyd couldn't hear her. Tammy's voice was drowned out by the loud whoop of the siren.

Fifteen minutes later, husband and wife sat handcuffed in the cruiser's back seat. The cops had opened the garbage bag and then reached for their side arms.

Both officers now stood behind the old station wagon, staring at the temporary tag. One of them turned toward Lloyd and Tammy, a huge grin on his face.

"Lloyd, honey?" Tammy's voice was very soft. "When you put that date on the temporary tag, what was it you wrote exactly?"

"Like I told you, Tammy, the last day of the month."

"And that would be?"

"Why, February the thirty-first. What else?"

Tammy just sighed and shook her head. So the cops had seen the date and stopped them on a whim. She wanted to weep, or even scream, but she couldn't be mad at Lloyd. To her knowledge, he'd never read anything in his life, and that included a monthly calendar. And she also remembered something she never should have forgotten. He was never any good at details.

Just Cause

Midnight, and a somber silence lay over second floor Homicide. Lightning glimmered through the grimy windows, followed by a low mutter of thunder. A row of overhead lights flickered and the air conditioner let out a groan. The burly detective with the bushy mustache listened and wiped sweat from his brow.

"Go ahead and quit," he growled. "You're not doing your job, anyway."

He glanced at his partner, seated at an opposite desk. The other policeman, his pale and intent face bent over a sheaf of papers, didn't respond. Finally, he raised his head and looked absently at his partner.

"Were you talking to me, Frank?"

"No Paul, I was speaking to the air conditioner."

The younger man shook his head and continued to read. A dark lock of hair fell across his forehead and he absentmindedly brushed it back. The rimless glasses, perched on his nose, gave him an earnest and studious appearance. After a moment, he removed the spectacles, sighed, and leaned back in his chair.

"So you got it," said Frank.

"Yep, full confession, signed, taped, and witnessed."

"Go figure it," said Frank. "Middle aged couple, married for years, husband a successful banker, and tonight she puts a .22 slug right through the middle of his forehead. I hope she told you why."

The younger man's thin lips twitched in something like a smile. "Yes, Cynthia was very forthcoming. She thinks she had just cause."

"Just cause," snorted Frank.

"What was it, another woman"?

"Other *women* would be more like it," Paul said. "It seems the deceased kept a continual affair going down at the old First National, a succession of young and gullible cashiers."

Frank shook his head. "And his wife a real looker."

"Yeah, and also strong minded," Paul said. "Told me her husband, Don, insisted they share a bedroom, but they'd used it for nothing but sleeping after she found out about the girlfriends."

"So that's it," said his partner, placing both broad palms on his desk. "She finally got fed up with Romeo and popped a cap on him."

"Oh, I'm sure she was fed up," answered Paul, "but she said she'd resigned herself to it long ago. After all, there was a son and daughter in college and other economic considerations. Big Don was working on his fourth million. But then he started to get abusive."

"Physically abusive?"

"Yeah, well nothing real extreme. He'd grab her arm sometimes or shove her out of the way when they met in the hall. But it was abuse all the same."

"I guess her cutting him off had started to wear on his nerves," said Frank.

"Maybe, but of course that's no justification. Anyway, Cynthia said she'd learned to deal with that, too. She simply tried to avoid him."

"By now, she must have really hated the guy."

"Yes," Paul said. "I suppose she did."

Frank gave his partner a sly look. "There's more to this, isn't there?"

"Not much more," Paul said. "The husband seems to fit a pattern, a self made man, full of his own importance, rich, selfish, and uncaring. He was also a control freak. His wife says he'd come home and pull *inspections*, for Pete's sake, line the servants up and make them follow him around the house. If he found a dusty shelf or a dirty dish, he'd ream them all out, her included."

"Well, that wraps it up then," said Frank, throwing both hands in the air. "You've seen it before and so have I. Cynthia took it all, the philandering, the abuse, the endless fault finding. Finally, she just lost it and reached for the pistol." He rubbed his face and stared at the man opposite him. The man opposite him slowly shook his head.

"Nope," he said.

"Oh, come on, Paul," exclaimed Frank, rising to his feet. "If you knew she had a separate motive, why'd you tell me all this other stuff?"

The younger man rose, also, and walked over to the

window. He stood looking down at the deserted street, his gaze following a candy wrapper, blowing along the sidewalk.

Finally, he turned and said, "Because the other stuff was a factor. Of course it was. It had to be, right?"

Frank started to respond but his partner held up a palm.

His face a study in perplexity, Paul exclaimed. "I mean, what she finally told me, the real reason she put a bullet through his brain, why, that was no reason at all. That wasn't even..."

"What the devil are you talking about, Paul?"

The young man didn't answer. Instead, he walked back to his desk and pulled open a drawer. He withdrew a plastic cassette and held it up to his partner.

"Cynthia gave me this," he said. "She wanted me to play it, wanted someone else to hear what Don had been doing to her."

Paul placed the cartridge into a nearby player and pushed a button. For a moment, they heard only the hissing reel. Then, a raucous noise rushed out through the speaker with a force and ferocity that made the player vibrate. It started at some deep groaning level and rose to a gurgling, whistling crescendo. After a second of expectant silence, it began again and repeated itself over and over and over. It was an alien sound, yet eerily familiar. Frank brought his hands to his ears.

"Turn it off," he cried.

"Keep listening," said his partner.

The racket continued for a moment more, and then the policemen heard a sharp explosion, like a firecracker going off. After that, came a deep and deathly silence.

Paul pushed another button and lifted out the tape.

His partner stared blankly at him. And then, across the older man's face, there passed a peculiar look, at once an expression of dawning understanding, yet growing disbelief.

"His snoring?" Frank said in a rising voice. She shot him because he snored? Naw, I ain't buying that, partner. It had to be the other stuff."

"She says not," answered Paul. "She was quite insistent about it. Said she'd been forced to listen to that sound for what seemed an eternity, *forced,* mind you, with no chance of escape. Remember, Don wouldn't allow separate bedrooms. She had endured it for years, and to imagine enduring it for the rest of her life, all those endless nights, well, that was unthinkable."

"So his snoring became the ultimate transgression."

"Well, you listened to it," Paul said with a dispassionate shrug. "It was, to say the least, intense."

"And she killed him for it," replied Frank. His voice held a note of wonder.

"I'm afraid so," Paul said. "Oh, don't be so incredulous, Frank. There have been stranger motives. As a married man, you should understand these things. You *are* still married, aren't you?"

"Still *happily* married," replied Frank.

"Glad to hear it," Paul said. "By the way, do you snore in your sleep?"

"I have no way of knowing," said his partner with a wry grin.

"Sure you do," Paul said. "Just ask your wife. It might help her to talk about it."

I Can't Get It Out of My Head

Harry Simpson stared at the words and notes and wondered if they'd work. OceanAire had loved his last advertising jingle and they'd paid well for it. That little ditty remained on TV and radio for a year. Proof of how much OceanAire thought of it was their request that he do another. And now, after laboring past midnight, he'd created it. Part of the tune went:

> For the lowest price in airline fare,
> Nobody's lower than OceanAire

Harry grinned ruefully at the lines and slowly shook his head. Practically anybody could accomplish this much. But few could have come up with the accompanying melody and that's what brought the simple language to life, not only brought it to life, but made it linger in the mind. And *that* was Harry's talent.

He placed his hands on the piano keys and, once more, played the notes. Close, but the ending needed emphasis. He was about to try again when he heard the car approaching. Earlier tonight, Harry had retreated into Crowley's Ridge to escape distractions and he listened to the car motor with a small frown of annoyance. Nobody knew this was his cabin so it couldn't be a visitor. The vehicle turned off the highway onto a gravel road, which ran by the cabin and into the hills beyond. The tires crunched past, and then the car stopped and the driver turned the engine off. Harry considered going outside to take a look, but thought better of it. He had a good idea who was in the car, two lovebirds looking for a secluded place to make out. Besides, he was concentrated on the tune. His fingers swept over the keys again, an eleven note refrain that grabbed your attention and kept it. After playing it once more, Harry decided he'd been wrong before. What could he say? It was perfect. He closed the cover on the piano, thinking how good his bed was going to feel. At the same time, he heard the car start up. It turned around on the gravel, reached the main highway again, and headed into the night.

Early next morning, Harry walked out on his front porch and took a deep breath of the clean, country air. He was about to go back inside when his eyes caught a spot of color on the gravel road. He descended the porch steps and walked toward it. The high-heeled slipper's green gloss contrasted sharply with the dirty gravel. Harry bent to pick it up. As he straightened, he noticed another shoe, sticking out of the bushes. It enclosed a woman's foot. The other foot lay pale and naked beside it.

Simpson sat on his porch, watching the sheriff and one of his deputies. The county coroner was with them. All three men were standing over the body. Sheriff McClain looked around and started toward the cabin. Harry observed the familiar shuffle. They had known each other for years.

McClain stopped by the porch and looked up. "Anything else you recall seeing or hearing?"

"No, Wilbur." Harry looked down at the ground. "I guess I should've gone outside."

McClain placed a foot on the step and gazed at his friend. "Had you done that," he said, "we might've found you lying beside her. Coroner says she's been dead for over twelve hours. That means she was killed, then brought out here. Nothing you could have done."

"How did she die?" asked Harry.

"Strangled."

"Oh, no."

"Yep, I think it's related to the others," said Wilbur. "Young woman, strangled and found on Crowley's Ridge. That's the third one in two years."

"Any clues at all?"

"None, but logic would tell you that the same person did all three, and it would also tell you that he lives around here."

Simpson returned to Medford in the early afternoon and realized he was hungry. After what he'd seen, a breakfast had been out of the question. He entered the Elite Restaurant, took a table by the front window, and ordered sausage and eggs. The hills of Crowley's Ridge rose in the distance and Harry gazed at them while he sipped his coffee. He felt the waitress's hand on his shoulder and looked up.

"Harry, you care if this gentleman sits with you? All the tables are full." A thin, balding man stood behind her, wearing an apologetic smile.

"Hope you don't mind," he murmured.

"No problem," said Harry. "Take a seat." He had a vague recollection of the man, a Frolic Garment Company supervisor, who'd transferred in a couple of years ago. "Harry Simpson," he said, extending his hand.

The man gave it a weak shake. "Sidney Reese," he responded.

Reese ordered a burger and fries. He sucked Coke through a straw, and like Harry, stared out through the window.

"Those hills are lovely, aren't they?" he said.

"Yes, they are," replied Harry.

"I like to drive through them. Sometimes I take a friend with me. It's so peaceful up there." Sidney's face acquired a faraway look. He began humming softly to himself, a lilting, eleven note tune.

Simpson's fork fell clattering to the table. The man gave him a quick look.

"Oh, sorry," he said. "I heard that melody last night and I just can't get it out of my head. Do you know it?"

"It's about an airline," Harry whispered.

"An airline?"

"Yes," said Harry.

"So it's a commercial," he said. "Well, I might have known."

The waitress brought the man's order and placed it on the table. Reese took a huge bite from the hamburger and chewed on it thoughtfully. "Gooood," he sighed, speaking with his mouth full.

Harry just nodded his head. He needed to go find Wilbur McClain. He needed to get up right now.

And he wondered if his legs would work.

The New Line

In the heart of New York's garment district stands a red brick building, its sides begrimed by soot. At the front, a metal sign proclaims: MARKOFF AND STYLES—FINE CLOTHING. Alfred Markoff and Billy Stiles founded the business, and on this Friday night in late November one partner lifted a glass to the other in the plush, thick-curtained dimness of Alfred Markoff's office.

"Here's to us, Billy. This year wasn't so great but the next one will be better."

Stiles lifted the glass to his lips and said, "I think it will be, Alfred."

"So what brings you to my office at this late hour? We're probably the only ones left in the factory."

"Well, not quite. There's a friend of mine outside. I'll call him in a minute."

Markoff's eyes narrowed. He walked behind his desk and set down the glass.

"Something on your mind, Billy?"

"Yes," said his partner. "It's you, Alfie. *You're* on my mind."

Alfred frowned and said, "What do you mean."

"I mean I know what you're doing, and I think I know when it started, sometime in August, wasn't it? That's when the casinos in Atlantic City called in your markers. You owe them big time, don't you Alfie, and you're paying them off with money stolen from the company, money stolen from *me*."

"Now just a minute, Billy. I don't know where you got the idea that I—"

"Save it, partner," said Stiles. "I know how to read ledgers, and I can tell when a profit statement is doctored. You and I are the only ones who could have done that, and I know it's not me. Right now, I'd say you've embezzled about $100,000, not bad for just a few months."

Markoff sank into his chair. "So what do you intend to do?"

"Well, I may have you thrown in jail," answered Billy. "I *could* you know. Alfred leaned forward and the knuckles of his right hand brushed against a desk drawer, the one where he kept his handgun. "But you're thinking of something else," he stated.

"Perhaps. At least you'd better hope so."

"And what is it you're thinking of, Billy."

Instead of answering, Stiles walked to the door and pulled it open. A tall, gray-haired man strode in. He moved over to a wall and stood silently, his eyes fixed on Markoff.

"Alfred, meet Phil Connors, my new partner."

"Your new what?" yelled Markoff, rising from his seat.

"You heard me," said Billy. "Now shut up and listen. You

will sell your share of the business to Mr. Connors and me. We'll pay you a fair price, less what you've stolen, and you will disappear forever from our sight. Is that understood?"

Alfred flopped in the chair and placed his hand on the drawer handle. "It'll ruin me," he muttered. "There won't be enough to start another business and I don't see myself behind a sewing machine."

Billy Stiles's voice held the finality of a judge passing sentence. "It's over, Markoff. Go home. Just be here Monday morning to sign the papers."

Alfred Markoff didn't have to think about it. He'd already made up his mind. Leaping to his feet, he yanked the desk drawer open, reached inside, and came up with the pistol. He swung it toward the two men and pulled the trigger twice. The first shot took Phil Connors in the middle of his chest, driving him against the wall. Stiles was heading toward him when the second shot tore into his shirtfront, blasting a button into flying fragments. He staggered backward and crumpled to the floor.

Markoff's brain burned and his whole body trembled. He felt sick to his stomach, but knew he'd have to think fast. The gun was untraceable but he needed to get rid of it. He stumbled into the bathroom, wiped off the pistol with a towel, and glanced about. A window opened onto the alley. Alfred thrust up the sash and looked down. An open-topped dumpster sat just below him. He took careful aim and let the weapon drop from the towel. It fell two stories and buried itself in the half-filled container. Alfred allowed himself a brief smile. He'd go home and wait for the police to call. They'd probably conclude the killer was some dope-crazed burglar. He turned to the bathroom doorway and stepped back into his office. A hoarse scream reached his ears and it took a second before he realized it was coming from his own throat. Billy Stiles and Phil Connors were coming across the office floor, their arms outstretched to grab him.

Phil explained it all to Alfred while they waited for the police. It was the first time he'd heard the man speak. The voice held a trace of Brooklyn.

"Well, I served with New York's finest for twenty years," he said, "but this is the first time I've ever been shot. Good thing I had the vest on."

"The vest?" whispered Alfred.

"Yeah sure, the bulletproof vest." Connors grinned and jerked his chin toward Stiles. "Your partner's wearing one, too. We were trying them on just before we came up to brace you. Didn't bother to take them off first. Good thing, huh, Billy?"

"A very good thing," answered Stiles.

Markoff found it hard to speak and his question came out in a croak. "Why in the world were you trying on bulletproof vests?"

Billy Stiles rubbed his chest and regarded his former partner with a look of anger and dismay, and maybe a trace of sadness. "Connors is the department's procurement officer. He came to me a while back with news the NYPD was looking to replace its outdated vests, all eighteen thousand of them. Well, its not our usual product but I told him we could handle it. Phil also announced he was nearing retirement. I'd just discovered what *you* were up to, so I told them that if we got the deal, he could come in with me. Tonight, he brought the contract along and quite a contract it is. Let's see, eighteen thousand vests at about five hundred dollars each. Well, you figure it out."

Billy was amused to see his partner actually trying to figure up the total in his head.

"So *that's* why were we trying on bulletproof vests, Alfie. It's our new line, and this vest, along with our other products, should put the firm of Stiles and Connors right back in the running. It's too bad you won't be around to see it.

Time Will Tell

Someone was stealing at table number six and that someone was a dealer. Solly Goldman knew this for a certainty, because after twenty-two years in the casino business, he'd learned that percentages never lie. Solly is General Manager of the El Dorado Casino. I'm one of his Pit Bosses and I know the same thing. Over a period of time, a blackjack table will give you, more or less, the same consistent profit. Yet, for the last three months, number six's percentage had dropped to the tune of $5,000 per month. This could not be, so Solly called me into his office and said:

"Okay Jimmy, here's the deal. We both know a dealer is knocking down at table number six, all right."

"Of course," I said, "that is accepted. The question is, which dealer?"

"Well," Solly said, "that's a question I suggest you find an answer to soon, because number six is in *your* pit."

"Solly," I said, "I'm doing everything I can think of. For two months, I've had the cameras trained on these dealers. I've reviewed about twenty miles of video tapes and they show me nothing."

"A smart dealer could hide it from the camera," Solly said. "He wouldn't have but a second, but he could do it if he's good."

"I know," I said, "so I've also watched from the pit. Security watches them, too. Nobody's noticed a thing."

"A dealer that's quick could hide the snatch from you," Solly said.

"I know," I repeated, "that's why I've had every one of them searched."

"You had them searched?' Solly said, raising his eyebrows.

"Yes I did. Okay, I know we may be getting into some legalities here, but what else we gonna do? We pulled a search on each dealer when they least expected it, and every time we turned up zilch."

Solly walked over to a wide, tinted window. I followed and we both stood looking down at the gaming floor and at table number six. It sat there, covered in green felt, seeming to mock us with its secret. I heard Solly let out a long sigh. He turned to me and said:

"Okay, get me Willie the Wizard."

Now in Las Vegas, there are lots of ways to catch a crooked dealer. First of all there's the cameras. They see all, they can see it in close-up, and they never blink. Then there's close observation by the Pit Bosses. We may blink, but we've seen every scam there is and we know what to look for. As a last measure, you can pull the dealer from the table and do a surprise search for chips. And if all this fails, you're left with two alternatives. You can fire every dealer at the table, or you can call in Willie the Wizard.

Of course, we all hate to bring in outside talent, but Willie got called a lot. Why? Simply because Willie was so *good*. She could watch a video tape or stand in front of a dealer and see what everyone else was blind to. The bosses said it was because Willie brought a fresh eye to the scene. I knew better, and I knew what her secret was. Willie was born with a gift.

She agreed to meet with us that afternoon and showed up at Solly's office around two o'clock. I let her in and watched her shake hands with Solly. I hadn't seen Wilhemina Riley in a couple of years, but she hadn't changed a bit. There stood the legend, a wispy little gray-haired lady, dressed in an elegant organdy dress. Around her delicate neck hung a strand of perfect pearls. She listened to Solly for a moment, then walked over to the video, pushed a button, and sat down to watch. Solly and I left her alone.

We were drinking coffee in the restaurant when my cell phone beeped and I fished it out of my pocket. I listened for a minute and turned to Solly.

"It's Willie ," I said. "She wants to see us."

We headed up to the office and Solly said, "No way can she know anything. We've only been gone thirty minutes."

Willie was standing at the window with Sol's binoculars, watching number six.

She turned to Sol and in a voice like somebody's grandmother said:

"Dear, who's that tall, thin dealer with the crew cut?"

Solly looked at me and I said, "That would be Tommy Reese."

"I think you should get him up here," said Willie.

And so it came to pass that while young Tommy Reese was climbing the stairs, Willie the Wizard walked over and switched the video back on.

"It's just luck that Tommy happened to be on this piece of tape," said Willie, "and convenient that he's working today."

She reached over and froze the tape. It showed a close-up of table six with the dealer's hands above it. "Look at the time on his watch," said Willie.

We both crowded over to look. The hands of the watch were quite visible on Tommy Reese's wrist. They read four o'clock.

"Now, I'll fast forward the tape.."

We watched the tape run, the dealer's hands a blur of motion. Willie pushed the stop button and we were looking at the watch again.

"I'd say I've run off about twenty minutes worth," Willie said.

The hands on the watch read four o'clock.

We were still staring at the screen when Tommy Reese opened the door. "You sent for me, Mr. Goldman?" he asked. He looked a little pale around the mouth.

"Yeah," Solly said. "I need you to answer a question for me?"

"Yes, sir, of course," the guy said.

"What time is it?" Solly asked.

Sweat appeared on Tommy's face and you could see his knees start to tremble. Solly just walked over, slipped the expansion band from Reese's wrist, and turned the watch over. We could all see that the back had been removed and that the whole watch was hollow. At least it *would* have been hollow had it not been for the $100 chip stuck inside.

I picked up the phone and called Security. They appeared and escorted Mr. Reese from the office. Solly held up the watch, dangled it in front of the Wizard, and said:

"Okay, Wilhemina, let's have the bad news. What's your fee gonna be for this one?"

"Now, Solly," said Willie, in that soft and oh-so-sweet voice, "did you hear me mention money?"

"Why no, Willie," Solly said, looking both pleased and surprised, " I guess I didn't."

And The Wizard said, "Well, I'm mentioning it now. You're going to have to lay it on me *heavy*."

Later that night, Solly and I were sitting in his office and Solly said, "You know, our Willie is a marvel. I watched those tapes a dozen times, and if I'd looked at them a hundred times more, I'd never have noticed that watch. Why is *she* the one who picks up on these things?"

"Maybe it's because she never takes anything for granted," I said, thinking Sol wouldn't want to hear what I really believed.

"You're wrong," said Solly Goldman. "That gal was born with a gift."

SCARY STORIES

"I will show you fear in a handful of dust."
—*T. S. Eliot*

The Children's Orchard

"It was growing dark and time to give up on my squirrel hunting. I wanted to get out of the woods while I could still see, so I started walking fast along the trail. The path made a sharp bend down the hill, and when I turned to follow it, I saw her there below me. She had on a white dress and she was looking up at me and smiling. I stopped dead still. I couldn't move another step 'cause, right away, I knew who it was. She stared at me a moment longer, then disappeared among the trees."

Here, Sam Ellison took a long breath and eyed his two companions.

"Who the heck did you see, Sam?" asked Big Ed Thompson, leaning back in his cane-bottomed chair.

"I saw my mother, Ed."

"What brought her out to the woods?"

"That I don't know," said Sam. "My mother had died eight years before."

"Uh-*huh,*" Big Ed said. "Well, I guess that tops mine about the ghost in the tractor shed."

All three men sat silently, for a moment, and stared at the flames in the fireplace, listening to the crackling wood and the moaning wind outside.

"How about you, Harry?" Sam asked. "You got a couple to tell us? That'll make two tales per man."

"I don't think so," Harry Johnson said, smiling at his friends. "Anyway, I don't think I could top you two."

"Well, you probably won't be as slick as old Sam," Ed said. "Notice how he brought his mother into the last one. You don't dare call him on it because that'd be like, you know, mocking his mother."

Sam looked at Big Ed and grinned. Friendship warmed them along with the fire. They'd built this cabin years ago and, despite their different backgrounds, had always gotten along. Of course, love of the outdoors and hunting were common bonds, but they were unalike in most everything else.

Big Ed was a farmer and a fairly prosperous one with all the fierce independence and gruff manner that are common to the breed. He loved hunting dogs and the land and the fellowship of other men.

Sam Ellison lived in Memphis and had for his entire working life been a postman, a simple, practical man, living in the eternal present and free from all ambition.

Harry Johnson was the only one of the three with a college education. He'd obtained a Master's Degree from Vanderbilt and gone on to teach English at a small college on the southern tip of Crowley's Ridge. His precise speech and cultured manner, so different from their own, was a constant source of amusement to Ed and Sam.

Now, as usual, the men found themselves together during the late deer season. A young buck, shot by Ed, hung from a tree outside, the carcass grown stiff from December cold and wintry wind. Blood had pooled and frozen beneath it, forming dark ice across the glistening snow. All about, the snowflakes drifted softly down into the woods of Crowley's Ridge.

The hunters were telling ghost stories, aiding their imaginations with an occasional pull from a jug of homemade wine. Sam had reeled one off about a haunted house and followed it up with the tale about seeing his dead mother. Big Ed's, bloodier than Sam's, told of an Indian chief, risen from the grave and back for revenge against the white despoilers of his land. Ed linked him to every unsolved murder around Crowley's Ridge for the past fifteen years.

Then, he'd told about the ghost in his tractor shed.

Big Ed farmed a large tract of land. He owned all kinds of equipment, and according to him, strange things began to happen in his tractor shed. Unexplained noises issued from it at night. Motor driven machines started up all by themselves.

One morning, a piercing scream brought Big Ed running from the main house. He found his hired man, Luke Dockery, face down in the shed with the back tire of a massive John Deere tractor resting on top of him. Luke's entrails, erupting out onto the dirt floor, gave proof of what that kind of weight can do to the human body.

The sheriff concluded that Luke, after starting the tractor, got down to check something. The brake slipped and one huge wheel rolled on top of the worker before he could move. Big Ed stared at both men with a rueful look on his face, as if to say, "I know otherwise."

"Well, come on Harry," said Sam, taking a swig from the wine jug. "Tell us a story."

Harry Wilburn eased forward in his rocking chair and stared into the fireplace. "I can't tell you a ghost story," he said. "I'm afraid I don't know any. But I can tell you something that happened to me once. At least, I think it happened."

A log settled lower into the flames, giving off sparks and a wisp of smoke.

"My grandmother, on my father's side, was Lucius Johnson's daughter and *Loosh* Johnson and his kin owned a big part of Crowley's Ridge. Johnsons lived all over the place and eventually they started their own cemetery. It's here on Crowley's Ridge, right out in the middle of the woods. Nobody gets buried there anymore, probably nobody even visits it anymore, but it's filled with nothing but Johnsons, all related to one another and all related to me. Well, I'd known about the place for years, but I'd never been there. About a year ago, I decided to pay a visit.

It was early morning when I started out and the weather had turned cold. To get where I was going, I had to take the gravel road that runs below the east side of the Ridge, the one they call the Low Road. I got on it and followed it toward the old deserted town of LaGrange. Low lying clouds covered the sky and I drove along with only the engine noise and the sound of tires on gravel to keep me company. Bare trees stretched out to either side. In that bleak light, they looked like something out of a dream. I remembered an uncle once told me to look for a dirt road with a big oak tree at the entrance. I finally saw both up ahead. When I reached them, I turned off.

The road turned out to be more like a trail. It ran up a hill and I could barely get my truck along it. At the top of the hill, the road ended. I got out of the truck and saw a faint path, winding down the opposite slope. I followed it on foot. The path entered a field of tall, dead grass, soaring up on either side. It reached well above my head, and as I walked along, I could only see as far as the next turn. Suddenly, the grass ended and I found myself standing at the edge of some woods. I glimpsed a clearing within the trees and followed the path toward it. Then, I saw the rough, gray tombstones and I knew I'd come to my journey's end."

Harry turned an ironic smile toward the others. "I remember feeling very excited," he said, "and glad I'd decided to visit."

I came up to the clearing and saw all the tombstones laid out in straight rows. Walking among them, I read some of the inscriptions. The name, Johnson, turned up everywhere, which didn't surprise me. It *was* surprising to see the place looking so well kept, because there was no sign of recent visitors.

I couldn't believe how quiet things were. Quietness seeped up out of the very ground. Dead leaves hung motionless on the trees without the slightest breeze to rustle them. The silence bore in on me, unbroken even by the call of a bird.

I looked up from the tombstones and glanced over to my left. Something interesting had caught my eye. Four small trees grew near the edge of the cemetery. Planted by someone long ago, they stood spaced in a row. They were fruit trees. I raise apples and peaches in my back yard and I saw the same trees here: apple-peach, apple-peach, all lined up. I walked over and stood looking up at the barren branches, twisting outward like someone's arthritic fingers."

Harry stared, for a moment, at the burning logs.

"You know how sometimes you see things and at first they don't register. Well, I had glimpsed something on the ground, but I'd looked at the fruit trees instead. Now, my eyes flew back to the ground again.

There they stood, little tombstones, scattered around my feet. They weren't in rows like the others, and they measured about one third the size. I knelt down among them.

One read: MATILDA–October 1919-December 1919.

On another it said: JEFFREY–June 1922-April 1930.

And on a third one: CYNTHIA–May 1904-November 1911.

My left knee began to ache and I realized it was resting on a concrete slab. I moved my leg around and brushed the dead leaves away. The slab was small, about one foot square, and three crude words, chiseled out by hand, took up all the space. They read: THE CHILDREN'S ORCHARD."

Harry spoke more softly and his voice seemed to come from a far off place.

"It's hard to explain," he said, "how those words made me feel. I guess some folks might have viewed the whole thing as thoughtful and nice, but I didn't feel that way at all. I knelt there and shivered in the cold, and all I could think was: *It's an orchard for dead kids.*

And did small children rise up out of these graves at the dying time of the year and lurch across withered leaves to reach up and pluck the rotting fruit?

"Get a grip on yourself," I murmured aloud. And the sound of my voice was startling in all that stillness. I stood up and took a few steps backward. The silence pressed in again, and for the first time, for no reason at all, I felt a stab of fear.

It was as if I'd become a boy again, walking alone at night down an empty dirt road, and hearing a sound at my back, but knowing I could not turn around, because if I did, I'd see that sharp-fanged, long-clawed monster of my nightmares. He'd have his hairy arms raised over his head and he would be creeping along, just behind me.

I forced myself to stand quietly for a moment, while my heartbeat slowed to normal. I glanced up at the motionless clouds. They hovered closer and they seemed darker than before. I glanced at my watch. It was time to go.

Then from behind me, ever so clearly, I heard a little girl's laughter.

It took all my will and effort to do what I had to do. I slowly turned around.

She stood off to the edge of the clearing, a child about seven years old, and she was smiling at me. Dark hair streamed past her shoulders. She was clothed in a one piece garment with a pink ribbon hanging down the front. The little girl remained motionless and so did I, while a horrible truth crept into my brain.

She was wearing a shroud.

Suddenly, giving another piping laugh, she ran across a corner of the cemetery and vanished into the woods.

For a moment, I stood petrified by fear. I couldn't lift my feet up. Then, with hammering heart and gasping breath, I managed to start moving toward the path. My only thought was to get out of there, to get *away*. But every step was a struggle, like wading in deep water. I tried desperately to go faster. I couldn't. And the certainty of what I'd seen now lay in my stomach like a block of ice. This had not been a living child who'd wandered from a house nearby. Her face had been as white as her shroud, and there *weren't* any houses nearby.

Oh, God, I thought, don't let her come back out of the woods. Don't let her come back out and stand in my way and wait for me. Just make her go back to her place in the ground. Thinking this, I jerked my head around. No, she hadn't returned to the Children's Orchard, but someone else stood there. It was a small blond-haired boy. He wore a little dark suit and one hand was thrust into a coat pocket. He leaned against a peach tree and regarded me with vacant, motionless eyes. His pallid face gleamed in the weak winter light. And then I heard his tinkling voice.

"I like it when kinfolk visit,"

Facing around, I stumbled forward and saw the path in front of me. I lunged along it through the woods and found myself within the tall grass again."

Harry gave his two companions a anxious look, as if to assure himself that they were still with him. He turned away and brought his chair closer to the fireplace.

"The worst part," he murmured, "was following that path through the high grass. I expected to see her around every bend. She'd be standing in front of me and then I'd turn around and see the little boy, coming up from behind with his arms stretched out.

They'd want to take me back to the Orchard so we could play.

Nothing appeared in front of me, though, and I didn't see the boy again. I *did* hear something. It came from off to the side, a rustling sound, staying even with me. Something out there, moving through the grass.

All at once, I broke into the clear and started up the hill. I saw my truck at the top. Stumbling up to it, I wrenched the door open, fell inside, and locked the door behind me. I pressed my face against the windshield and looked back down the path. Nothing was moving below. I started the engine and tried to put the pickup in reverse, but my hands had gone out of control. They didn't shake, they just *fluttered* all over the place. Finally, I found the gearshift lever and slammed it in reverse. I shot backward, swung the tail end around, and slid to a stop. And then, as I prepared to go forward, I heard three soft taps on the window beside me.

A lifetime passed. I couldn't move. And that dreadful sound reached me again. *Tap! Tap! Tap!*

It took all the strength within me to turn toward that window, but I had to look, I had to turn and look. I knew that if I didn't, I'd remain there forever, always and forever, frozen and staring out my windshield, listening for eternity to that awful, patient tapping on the glass.

She stood just outside. I knew she would be. The little, cold face pressed close, but the eyes, thank God, weren't staring at me. They were looking down at her hands, and her hands were on my door latch.

I groaned aloud and then heard myself saying in a thin, beseeching voice, *Oh, please go back. You need to get back to the Orchard.*

She retreated a few steps and stood staring at the ground. Then, with eyes still lowered, she slowly turned away. I pressed down on the gas and drove back toward the Low Road. Not once, did I look in my rear view mirror.

Darkness had fallen when I pulled into my driveway. The porch light cast a warm glow over the yard and I heard soft music playing in the living room. I thought that I had never seen or heard anything quite so comforting. *This* was tangible. This was real. And I began to think of the other thing as nothing more than a delusion, or perhaps a waking dream.

    I was halfway to the porch steps when it came to me that I hadn't locked my truck. I turned around, walked back to the driver's side, and took out my keys. Then I decided I wouldn't bother with it tonight. A pink ribbon, tied in a bow, was hanging from the door latch. It seemed a shame to disturb it.

A chill had settled into the one-room cabin and Big Ed went out to get more firewood. He returned with an armload and soon flames were leaping up the chimney again. The hunters gazed into the fire, which glowed on their faces and cast huge shifting shadows on the walls around them. Outside, the wind died down and the snow fell thicker and faster. It came down in great, drifting flakes, piling up on the cabin roof and covering Big Ed's footprints to the woodpile.

    Falling across a hundred miles of Crowley's Ridge, it filled up the valleys and lay across the hilltops and made the tree limbs droop with its weight. Some of the snowflakes settled on a bottomland lake and were swallowed up by cold, black waters, while others swirled across the deer trails and moved in solemn sheets along the Low Road.

    Down and down they drifted and filled up the night and fell softly on the Children's Orchard. And softly fell on the little boy and girl, standing with upturned faces among the tombstones.

    The snowflakes floated into their immovable eyes.

There's a Basement in the Arcade

Donald and I had worked all day in the vacant Central Station Building, hard dirty work, carrying out garbage and all kinds of debris and tossing the crap into a row of dumpsters. We finished the ground floor about seven o'clock and walked outside. The long days of summer were only a pleasant memory. Late October had come and the cold, damp air touched us like a clammy cloth. Heavy, dark clouds hung just above the rooftops. Across South Main Street, the windows of the Arcade Restaurant glowed with warm light and I could see people moving around inside.

"Hey Don," I said, "let's walk over and get a cup of coffee."

"Naw, I don't think so."

I glanced at Don and noticed he was giving the cafe a hard look, like he'd seen something he didn't like.

"Come on," I insisted, "some coffee will take the chill out of us."

Donald kept eyeballing the restaurant. "Did you know there's a basement in that place."

"Now how the hell would I know that," I replied? "Let's go get that coffee."

I was halfway across the street when I realized I was walking by myself. I looked back and saw Don standing on the sidewalk, still staring. He noticed me and sort of shook himself. Then he walked across the street and followed me through the door. We picked out a booth near the left wall and slid behind the table. An old black woman brought the coffee and we both took a sip. Donald sat facing the kitchen at the rear, looking like a cornered rat.

"What's the matter with you?" I asked.

Don just shook his head and gazed past my shoulder.

I leaned back and looked around. A row of tables ran down the center of the restaurant and a long counter lay just beyond them. To the right of the counter, a wide passage led into another room. I knew from past visits that this was sort of a poor man's ballroom where knockabout bands came to play and people gathered to drink. Like the rest of the building, it had seen better days. From the ragged linoleum floor to a cracked and water-stained ceiling, the whole musty, time worn, place reflected a tired endurance.

"It's a long while since I've visited the old Arcade. How about you?"

"Two and half years," Don answered, "and it still seems like a dream."

I looked at my buddy and set my cup down. "Donald Eugene, we might as well order some more coffee, because you are *gonna* tell me what the hell is bugging you."

Don took a big swallow of the fresh coffee; he didn't

seem to notice the stuff was steaming hot. Finally, he leaned back, licked his lips, and started talking.

"Last time I was in here," he said, "the Arcade was owned by another guy, called himself Tillman. He'd just taken the place over and needed somebody to clean out the basement. He offered me a hundred dollars to do the job. Also, I got to keep whatever was down there. The job had to be done after closing so as not to bother the customers. We shook hands on it and I left.

I showed up with my bob truck on a Wednesday night, just as Tillman was about to lock up. The deal was I'd keep the key to the back door, which opened out on an alley, and give it back the next day.

'You sure there's nothing you want to keep?' I asked him.

'Yeah, I'm sure,' he said. 'Hell, I don't even know what's down there. All I know is, I need the space. I got lots of new equipment coming in and it has to be stored. I ain't got time to sort through a bunch of junk.'

Well, I could tell he was in a hurry so I took the key and Tillman took off. I backed my truck up the alley, parked it, and unlocked the building's rear entrance. I walked down a narrow hallway and opened the basement door. Rough, wooden steps, hollowed out by a lot of use, sank into the dark. I flipped a wall switch and two naked light bulbs came on below me. I reached the basement floor and looked around. There wasn't much light, but I figured it was enough for what I needed to do. First thing, I looked to see if everything could be got up the stairs. To my relief, there was only carrying size junk. Most of it was just trash: old newspapers, cardboard boxes, empty bottles, a few beat up chairs. But in one corner, I noticed something shoulder high and about half as wide. It was draped with a dirty, mildewed quilt. Aw man, I thought, it's probably a damn refrigerator. I walked over, brushed away some cobwebs, and yanked off the cover."

For a moment, Donald's eyes held a faraway look, seeing once again what lay beneath the quilt.

"It was a jukebox," he continued, "an old-timey jukebox, the kind where you put a quarter in and a metal arm swings around and picks up a record. Well, the first thing I thought was, I'll never get it up the stairs. Then, it came to me that I might be looking at some money. This thing was definitely an antique and everything down here was mine. I wondered if it still worked. There was a cord curled around the bottom, and as luck would have it, a receptacle in the wall next to it. I plugged the jukebox in. Some interior lights flickered on and the plastic housing lit up and turned all the colors of a rainbow. And bubbles rose up through the housing, drifting through the bright colors.

It was beautiful.

I pushed a button, not bothering to read the selection. The arm swung around, picked up a record, and placed it on the spinning platter. And what came out of the speakers was an old Travis Trumbo song: 'Just Past Midnight.'"

In a high-pitched voice, my partner started to sing.

When the time is just past midnight,
Past time to be taking you home.
I wish we could stay here forever,
And live in this moment alone.

Don stopped singing and sat for a moment with his head down. Then he looked at me with eyes clouded in bewilderment. "And here's the part that seems like a dream. As soon as that song started playing, from the very first note, that old basement began to change. At first, things just felt different. Then, all at once, the air got colder and darker."

"Oh, stop the nonsense, Don," I said.

But Donald didn't stop. I don't think he even heard me. And I don't think he *could* stop. He'd become like that jukebox in his story, just playing his song.

"I don't mean the room got darker," he said. "The two bulbs burned just as bright. No, the *air* did and I could see it. I mean, I could *see* it slowly swirl and flow, like murky currents of water.

Then, I began to see other things.

A boy and girl appeared and danced out toward the center of the basement, moving with the music, and paying no mind to the garbage laying around. A stack of milk crates stood in front of them and they just swayed through it. But that didn't surprise me, because I could see through *them*.

Near a pile of moldy newspapers, another couple sat at a transparent table and drank malts and laughed in each other's faces. Or I guess they were laughing; that's what it looked like, but they didn't make a sound. Three guys stood by a wall and they were talking away, but I couldn't hear a word. Everything was silent, except for that song on the juke box.

I wish we could stay here forever,
And live in this moment... alone.

My buddy's voice died away; his vacant eyes stared into mine, and I realized that if Don wasn't telling the truth, he darn well *thought* he was.

"That song played on," he said, "and those see-through people danced and laughed and talked, like colorless figures in a silent movie. I stood there like a statue, unable to move, and off in far corners, I saw more ghosts, partying away like any kids would who were out on the town. And I knew it had to be a town of the early fifties, because all the girls were dressed in full skirts, puffed out with cancan slips, and they wore white bobby sox with their shoes. Yeah, they were having a high old time, like they'd probably had more than a half-century ago in this place. Mister Trumbo sang away and those phantoms kept moving around and it was then I decided to do some moving of my own. I double timed up the stairs, jumped in my truck, and drove off. And until tonight, I've never been back to the Arcade."

"Man oh man," I said. "That's some story. What about the basement?"

"What about it?" said Don.

"Well, you agreed to clean it out and you still had the key. Didn't Tillman try to get hold of you?"

"No, he never did, and I sent him the key through the mail. He didn't last long, anyway, kept the place for a couple of months and sold it to somebody else."

"How do you know?"

"The new owner called me up, said he'd talked to Tillman about our agreement, and offered me twice as much to do the same thing. I told him no deal."

Well, while Donald is telling me all this, you *know* what I'm thinking. If there's any truth at all to his story, that jukebox should still be down there, so I mentioned it and he says:

"Nope, not anymore."

"Why not?" I asked.

"Because it's right behind you," he said.

I looked straight at Don and the back of my neck turned cold. I slowly twisted around, and there it was, setting in a corner by the kitchen. The overhead lights reflected across its surface, lighting up the rainbow colors.

"The guy mentioned he was gonna bring it up," said Don, "said that was one thing I wouldn't have to fool with. I told him I still wasn't interested, but you know, I had to find out, so I asked him if he'd played it. The guy said no. As a matter of fact, he'd cut the cord off, said he just wanted it for a tourist attraction."

"Good thing," I said.

"Yeah," murmured Don, "good thing."

He and I finished our coffee and got up from the table.

"Let's go look at it," I said.

Don slowly shook his head.

I left him at the front door and walked back toward the kitchen. The jukebox waited there, silent and unlit. I wiped a sprinkle of dust from the window and looked down at the turntable. On it lay an old record. The label was stained and faded, but I could make out the title *and* the name of the artist.

It occurred to me, of course, that Donald had visited here previously, seen the jukebox with its record, and concocted his story. I looked back over my shoulder. My friend's pale face was *not* that of a man enjoying a joke. He frowned at me and jerked his thumb toward the door. I took a last look round the Arcade and saw only its visible forms, solid and familiar. The exception, of course, was the jukebox. It sat there like some haunted and sepulchral monument, ready to play a record for its own *particular* audience.

And I sensed, I *knew*, that at this moment, just beyond the periphery of my perception and human understanding, there stood a party of boys and girls. They had gathered in a place where it's always just past midnight and the air is cold and dark and moving in aqueous currents. And they were waiting, patiently and eternally waiting for their summons.

It would come. It would come. Sooner or later that record would turn, and once again, Old Travis would sing his song.

GREAT OUTDOORS

"The bluebird carries the sky on his back."
—Henry David Thoreau

Bushytails

I have long hunted squirrel on Crowley's Ridge and I can tell you that the gray squirrels dwell high on the Ridge itself, while the fox squirrels, those of the reddish tinge, are found along its base. Neither will go where the other one lives and no one knows why this is so.

Gray squirrels are smaller with less meat on their bones. Fox squirrels are plump and more sought after by hunters. I usually hunt the gray squirrels because I like to hunt up high and gray squirrels contribute more to the quest. They are faster and more agile. They are harder to locate. I think they are more adventurous.

A gray squirrel, upon sighting you, will sit on his tree limb and scold you with a chirruping kind of bark, and will keep it up until you bring the rifle to your shoulder. Then, he'll seem to disappear, moving so fast you won't see him go. Suddenly, he'll show up on another limb, hunched down with his forepaws held in front, and scolding you again. That second scold could be his last if you are ready with your rifle, and wise in the ways of gray squirrels.

On Crowley's Ridge, it's easier to walk along the ridge tops because there is little undergrowth, and more often than not there are paths. And the grays are often found there. They love the higher places. They also love the hickory trees, which grow on top of the ridges and furnish them with their staple food, the hickory nut.

To hunt grays, you should possess a certain amount of patience, because they cannot be pursued. Their hearing and sight is very keen and they will hear or see you long before you detect them. You must therefore find a likely hickory tree, or better still a *grove* of hickory trees, and then wait patiently. By all means sit. The lower you are to the ground, the less visible you will be and the less movement you will produce. Squirrels, like all wild animals, zero in on movement. Be still and listen. You will sometimes hear the gray before you see him. He may give that unmistakable chirrup or you will hear his claws scratching against the tree bark. Since he is often holding a hickory nut, he sometimes drops it, and the sound of it falling through the tree limbs is a dead giveaway. Look upward and you may see him peering down, looking for his lost treasure.

Probably the first thing you glimpse will be his tail. Fleecy and long and lucent, it curves up and outward from his body and waves to and fro like a silver standard. And in homage to this appendage, the gray (and his foxy cousin) have long been called the bushytails.

Early morning and late afternoon are the best times to hunt them. It is then that they feed. Usually during the day, and always at night, they are at home in their nests. These are similar to those that birds build, but are larger and comprised only of twigs and sticks. It's considered bad form to shoot into these nests, even it you see a feathery tail protruding over the edge.

My rendezvous with grays is usually during the early hours. This morning, I approach a certain grove of hickory trees before the sun appears. The eastern sky is pale, but above me distant stars still twinkle, and in the lingering darkness I must yet be careful where I place my feet. I come up to the nearest hickory tree and walk past it into the center of the grove. A large tree stands before me and around its base grows a carpet of soft moss. I lean my back against the tree and slide down to a sitting position. Stretching my legs out in front, I lay my rifle across them.

The hunters of bushytails carry either shotguns or rifles. The shotgun hunters believe that their guns, though short on range, are more effective when fired into thick leaves and branches and they are right. The rifle hunters are more trusting in their aim and value the extra distance their weapons give them. And they love to track their targets, traveling along distant limbs. I am a rifle hunter.

The little .22 lying across my knees feels very light and my own weight seems diminished by the cushion of moss I rest on. All is quiet. There is no wind and not a leaf flutters. I lean my head against the tree and watch the eastern sky brighten while the hickory grove takes on light and color and depth. The trees reach upward to a great height, and their golden leaves, touched days ago by frost, glimmer softly against the sky. I sit still and wait.

Chiiirrruuup! The sound, coming off the silence, acts like an electric prod against my backbone and I straighten beneath the tree. My hand creeps to the rifle and I slowly peek around. The squirrel's bark has come from directly in front, but the trees seem empty. Then, off to my left, something begins to fall, clicking against a succession of branches. I have heard this sound before. It can only be a hickory nut. I believe I've spotted the tree, which stands by itself and is taller than the rest. The thick trunk seems to go up forever and great limbs sweep outward, flush with myriad branches and amber leaves.

My eyes search the tree a limb at a time, starting at the top and working toward the base. I'm halfway down, and even though a spot of gray appears in my vision, it does not at first register. Then my eyes fly back to that spot of gray.

The bushytail sits in profile on an outer limb. His paws are held in front and they clasp a hickory nut. His tail fans out in an arc behind him. I slowly bring the rifle to my shoulder and raise my knee so that my left elbow can rest on it. I have him in my sights. I bring the barrel down a bit until the front bead rests on the squirrel's shoulder. I take a deep breath, let out half of it, and slowly squeeze the trigger.

CRAAACK! The Marlin jolts against my shoulder, and over its barrel I see the gray fly out from the limb and tumble downward, hitting the ground with a soft thump. I mark where he lands and lay the rifle back across my knees. I have not forgotten the gray who barked a moment ago. The rifle shot has scared him and caused him to hide, but I know that if I'm patient he'll soon show himself. Squirrels do not have memories.

Swatches of sunlight lie across the forest floor and a welcome warmth is replacing the morning chill. A crow flies over, disrupting the silence with his harsh squawk. I watch a mass of leaves flutter under a slight wind and then grow still again. As I gaze upward, the leaves move once more but the motion this time is different. They and the branches supporting them have begun to jerk and quiver. Finally, a small gray head pokes through. The bushytail springs to an adjoining limb and is preparing to scramble along it when my bullet catches him. His fall seems slow and somehow graceful as he descends through the air, his tail streaming behind him.

I gather up both squirrels and start back toward the main road. I always consume what I take in the woods and two are enough for a meal. The path winds and descends before me and my stride lengthens. The sun now warms my bones and the forest gives off a musky autumn scent and the grays make a comforting weight in the back of my hunting vest. Another squirrel runs across a lofty limb, but he is safe for today.

Tonight, I will eat of the squirrels that ate of the hickory nuts, and I will think back on this morning's harvest and remember the hickory grove in pearly light and how the bushytails looked, scampering among the treetops.

And the memory of all this will be seasoning for my supper.

Across The Levee

Below the Missouri line, stretching to the southern and western horizons, is the Arkansas portion of the vast Mississippi Delta. Along the eastern side flows that enormous river, rolling its mile-wide current down to the Gulf of Mexico. And running parallel with this stream, to protect the delta farmers from annual floods, is a high earthen dike called a levee. The strip of land between the levee and the river, where flooding still occurs, is covered in virgin timber and is much the same as it was a hundred and fifty years ago when Mark Twain piloted past it in a steam boat.

The raccoon, or "coon," has long thrived in this country, despite coon dogs, trailed by their owners, who come by night to pursue him down his familiar paths until he is forced to take refuge in, and is subsequently shot out of a tree.

These coonhounds come in four breeds: the Bluetick, the

Black and Tan, the Redbone, and the Walker. They are similar in that they are all built large, have flopping hound ears, give the long, coarse (some say beautiful) bay of the hound, and possess an amazing sense of smell. The difference is in their coloring and perhaps in their reputations. The Bluetick is thought to have the keenest nose, and the Black and Tan, as well as the Redbone, are known for their affectionate nature. The Walker, largest of the breeds, is valued for the one quality that all coon hunters give him. The Walker, they say, will never ever give up on a scent.

Their adversary, the coon, is of only one breed and one description. He stands about a foot high, is generally the color of wood smoke, and flourishes a long bushy tail. This tail is circled with dark rings. An equally swarthy mask of fur surrounds the coon's eyes and makes him look like a four-legged felon. He is quick, agile, and fearless, and although much smaller than his opponent, can, when cornered, whip any coonhound that ever lived.

My grandfather was a coon hunter, and on a November night in earlier days when I was of a more tender age and he was still alive, we crossed the levee on a coon hunt. This was my first time hunting and I remember we stood for a moment at the edge of the black woods with the levee looming behind us and a pale moon streaming cold light upon us and we both breathed in the frosty night scent of the forest.

My grandfather turned on a light, strapped to his forehead, and I flipped the switch on my flashlight. Their beams cast two glowing spots on the forest wall. We both wore heavy hunting coats, thick pants, and lace-up boots. I carried a .22 caliber rifle and he held a .12 gauge shotgun. He also held a leash, which restrained our one coon dog, a large Walker my grandpa had chosen to name Joe Cobb. The old man, called so by all his sons and grandchildren, looked at me and smiled.

"You ready to go?" he asked?

"Yes sir, I'm ready," I replied.

He reached down, unsnapped the leash on Joe's collar, and we moved into the woods. I felt as if I'd left a lighted room and entered a dark basement. Overhead, the thick foliage shut off the moon glow and left us dependent on our light beams. These reflected off huge tree trunks, reaching upward and out of sight. Joe Cobb trotted a few yards ahead and began quartering back and forth. Several brief whines escaped through his nostrils. Then, he bounded out of sight and we heard only short yelps, sounding from different places.

"He's searching," the old man muttered.

"Why is he barking like that?" I asked.

"He's coming across other scents, maybe a squirrel or a deer. He won't follow 'em."

"Why not, Grandpa?"

The old man patted me on the shoulder. "Because he's a coon dog," he said.

Joe's outcries faded in the distance and we quickened our pace. The woods were free of undergrowth so we walked without hindrance through the trees. I couldn't hear the dog anymore and I cast an anxious look at my Grandpa. The old man just kept plowing ahead. Then, a series of barks reached us and we came to a stop.

"I think he's struck a coon trail," my grandfather declared.

My heart beat faster and I ran past him toward what had become non-stop barking. I heard the old man's soft chuckle as he followed along. Moments later, we came to a clearing, covered in dead grass and lustrous with moonlight. I could easily see Grandpa's dog on the other side, peering into the farther woods and barking furiously. He heard us and looked over his shoulder, his eyes fixed on my grandfather. I sensed he was waiting for something.

"Yeeeee!" rose a clarion voice from beside me. "Get'em, Joe Cobb."

With that, the great dog leaped into the forest and was instantly lost from sight. Then, my grandfather and I heard the first of that long, deep-throated baying. It hung and resonated in the air and brought a chill to my backbone. I have since heard that sound described as mournful. That was not what it was at all. On that night, Joe Cobb's bay was full of excitement, full of hope. He had finally struck his proper trail.

The old man and I kept our light beams pointed ahead and moved as quickly as we could through the darkness. The hound ranged toward the right and we headed in that direction. Several times he crossed back and forth in our front and each time we cut across and shortened the distance. Joe's voice kept coming like a long, lone note, blown on an oboe, drawing us onward.

Abruptly, the baying ceased and there was no sound except the wind, sloughing through the treetops. The silence came on so suddenly, it brought us to a stumbling stop. Then, the short yelping began, sounding just as it had when we stood in the clearing, and the old man said, "He's treed him."

We hurried forward, circled a clump of hackberry bushes, and finally caught sight of Grandpa's dog.

The hound stood on his hind legs with both forepaws

braced against the rough bark of an oak tree. He was looking up into its branches and barking with unrestrained fury. Every few seconds his back feet would leave the ground as he leapt upward toward his prey.

"Joe Cobb," the old man yelled and the dog settled back on his haunches. He ceased barking but continued to stare upward, his body tense and expectant. My grandfather walked over and patted his hound on the head, and I heard him murmur, "Good dog. Good dog, Joe Cobb." I let the beam of my flashlight travel slowly up the tree trunk, and about halfway to the top, on a stout, bare limb, crouched an animal. The old man was still petting his dog.

"Grandpa," I said, "there he is."

He strolled over and we both stood gazing up at the reason for it all. The raccoon looked down at us, his eyes reflecting fire from our light beams. The long, ringed tail trailed under the limb, swept forward by the wind. Squirrels were the only animals I'd seen in trees before and I was surprised at the size of this bulky animal with his thick, blowing fur.

"Better shoot him down now," said my grandpa.

I looked around, taken aback by his words. I hadn't considered this part of the hunt. My rifle remained at my side and I couldn't seem to lift it. I just stared at the old man.

"They're awfully good when you bake 'em with sweet potatoes," he declared.

I continued to stare and he placed his hand on my arm and said in a gentler tone, "It's what we came for. It's what the dog expects."

I looked at the quivering hound, his eyes still fixed on the raccoon in the tree, and I knew what Grandpa meant. He was trained for a great coonhound and he must have it all. I was also aware of my own excitement, gradually building, and a single glance at my grandfather told me he was one with me and Joe Cobb.

We all looked toward our quarry and I slowly raised the rifle to my shoulder.

Jugging With Bubba

In Life On The Mississippi, Mark Twain wrote that the Indians believed a demon inhabited the river and that its roar could be heard for a great distance. Twain continued: "I have seen a Mississippi catfish that was more than six feet long and weighed two hundred and fifty pounds and anyone seeing such a fish has a fair right to think that the river's roaring demon has come."

It is generally accepted that jug fishing is a southern sport. It may be practiced in northern climes, but its birthplace is in Dixie. And it is always done on a river, preferably a wide river with a steady current.

You need a couple of dozen plastic gallon milk jugs, capped so they're watertight, and painted with a paint that won't wash off. Black shows up best against a sun-brightened surface. Knot one end of a ten-foot length of heavy fishing line to each jug handle. On the other end of the line, tie off a large fishing hook and mount a lead weight or "sinker" just above it. Now, all you lack is the bait. It should be something rotten and evil smelling because you are after river catfish and this is what they love. The bait of choice is bits of raw meat ripened under a hot sun. Catfish are especially partial to chicken.

Bubba Hansen jug fishes on the Mississippi in the early spring, when catfish are most active. He uses a fourteen-foot metal johnboat boat, devoid of frills or comforts. Bubba is tall and lean and weathered. Most of his years have been spent outdoors and frills or comforts are not a priority. However, a modern thirty horse Mercury outboard is attached to the stern of his simple boat. He will need its power to forge against the mighty river's current and to keep tabs on the shifting, drifting jugs.

With jugs and bait aboard, Hansen shoves off from an Arkansas sand bar. The motor grumbles pleasantly as he backs out and swings the boat northward. He flips the gear lever to forward, twists the throttle, and heads upriver. His pickup truck, parked high on the bank, shrinks in the distance. Twenty miles ahead of him lies Plum Point, where the Mississippi makes one of its many bends. Bubba will throw out his jugs at that point of land and let them drift southward. The trick is to reach his pickup truck at the same time he is done fishing. From past visits to Plum Point, he knows that this will take about three hours, plenty of time to capture some of the river's big cats.

Bubba stays close to the Arkansas shore, where the current is less powerful. He leans back against the outboard motor, letting his hand rest lightly on the combination throttle and steering handle. The little boat surges along, leaving a bubbling wake. The Mercury's low growl permeates the nearby woods, causing flocks of blackbirds to pour out of the trees and swoop and swirl above Bubba's head. He can smell the rain soaked forest, rich with new growth, and the sweet, musky scent of honeysuckle. Finally, Bubba spies Plum Point and angles out toward the center of the river.

The twenty jugs lie in two rows at his feet. All lines are baited and stretched out straight. Bubba plows back toward the Arkansas shore at a slower pace. Every ten yards he tosses one of the jugs overboard. When the final jug hits the water, he makes a sweeping right turn, throttling down when he is upstream from the array. The sun is well up on Bubba's left and its morning rays glint and sparkle on the river surface. The black jugs stretch from left to right, looking like watery holes in the river. They and Bubba and his boat sweep southward together.

The jugs start drifting apart. Some speed up or slow down in the inconstant current. Bubba guns the Mercury to full power and dashes to the left perimeter. He picks up six errant jugs and heads back along the row, dropping a jug where a space has formed. Then he resumes his station behind the shortened line. Movement on the right catches the fisherman's eye and he looks over in time to see a jug bobble in the water. He remains motionless and watches it. Waves might be causing the movement. Suddenly, the jug upends and begins to sink. Instantly, Bubba gives the motor full throttle and the johnboat bow rises high in the air. Other jugs flash by him as he races toward the one that's half submerged. The jug travels a few feet upstream and all doubt about what moves it is gone. Something has taken the bait.

The johnboat rushes up to the jug and Bubba cuts the

motor. He grabs the plastic with both hands and heaves upward. The visible line strains and trembles. He reaches out with a gloved hand and pulls up a length of it. Just beneath the surface, he sees a shadowy shape knifing back and forth. He grabs another handful of the line, stands up in the boat and gives a final heave. The catfish bursts from the water and flies into the boat. It flops and struggles, the smooth skin wet and glistening. Bubba takes a small hammer and strikes it between the eyes. The catfish stiffens and grows still.

Hansen re-baits the hook, looks up, and sees that he's drifted in front of his line. He points the little boat upstream and gets behind it again. On the way through, he drops off the newly baited jug.

Tending the group becomes a nonstop job. Bubba dashes from one end to the other, like a border collie herding sheep. When the jugs get too dispersed, he moves them closer together. Occasionally, a jug will begin to bob and sink and Bubba races over to retrieve the catfish. A few escape the hook, but in a couple of hours he has brought six more into the boat. It's a good haul. The fish average over ten pounds apiece.

Blackbirds still circle above, watching the boat and its occupant in the stern. They see it dart in and out among the dark objects, throwing up a sparkling spume, the outboard snarling and roaring. The show drifts southward beneath them and the blackbirds follow along.

Bubba sweeps by a familiar grove of oak trees and realizes he's getting close to home. He stretches out his legs and pops open a can of Coors. The jugs have arrayed themselves into a loose cluster, and for the moment, are keeping together. A fresh breeze skims across the water, rippling its surface and drying the sweat on Bubba's face. He takes a deep swallow of beer and lets his eyes wander once more over the cluster of jugs.

Yes, the one nearest to him has definitely moved, turning upside down in response to a tug on the line. The jug rights itself and drifts along with the others. He continues to watch. A huge, dark form appears below the jug and slowly sinks from view.

Bubba blinks and shakes his head. He isn't sure he's seen this. And then the jug he's watching dives beneath the surface. It simply disappears and doesn't come up again. Bubba looks quickly around the boat. The jug is nowhere in sight. This is something outside his experience. He has never known a fish to completely submerge a gallon jug and keep it under this long. Suddenly, a few yards downstream, the jug plops to the surface. Just as quickly, it goes under again. Bubba judges where it will next appear and races to the spot. Looking down, he sees the jug traveling just below the water's face. He reaches beneath it, pulls upward . . . *and remains frozen.* The thing towing the jug cannot be budged. As a matter of fact, Bubba now feels himself being pulled toward the water. He steadies himself and stops the movement, but he can't pull the line up, not even an inch. Whatever is at the other end is easily holding its own. Bubba braces for another heave, but the line suddenly slackens and he realizes the creature is gone. He brings the jug and line aboard and stares at the hook on the end. It is almost straight, the curve pulled out with effortless strength.

Bubba is still staring at it when something rubs against the bottom of the boat, causing it to rock in the water. He peers over the side and takes in a sight that will always be a part of his memories.

The massive catfish swims very near the surface and is quite near to Bubba. He is almost as wide as the boat and he is keeping pace with it, swimming along with unhurried ease. The great head trails a foot long whisker on either side, and as Bubba watches, the catfish swings slowly toward him and draws closer to the boat. The wide-set eyes look upward through the water, and for a moment, fish and fisherman contemplate each other. Then, the catfish begins to sink, slowly descending, and Bubba watches it go down and keeps gazing into the depths long after his fish is gone.

Bubba rounds the final bend and sees his pickup in the distance. He sets about the task of gathering and securing his jugs. That done, he points his craft toward the western bank. The seven fish lay at his feet. Bubba glances at them, but he is thinking of another fish. He picks up the outsized hook, which is no longer a hook, and holds it in his palm. It lies there, naked and gleaming, mocking him with its shape, and reminding him of that which was lost.

Bubba closes his eyes, and for a moment, sees the catfish again, heading toward him, moving with casual power and an utter lack of fear. He looks back over his shoulder, back across the far reaches of the Mississippi, and imagines the great fish down in the river's depths, deep down where all is black and cold, drifting alone midst an ocean of sweeping water.

And then he suddenly smiles. A realization has just crept in, amusing to him since it is so contrary to his nature. It has just occurred to Bubba Hansen that he's glad this fish is where it is and not held captive on his line.

Shanging

Searching for ginseng, or *shanging,* in the Arkansas hills is like digging for diamonds near Murfreesboro. The state offers both items but they are in short supply and the chance of finding them is remote. The ginseng root is no diamond, but when you consider that the prime article sells for $500 a pound, you will understand why "shang" has been depleted.

It once grew along the entire expanse of eastern America, and from the very first, its value was known and it was dug up wherever found. As a result of this pillage, the modern searcher may liken himself to a certain gallant knight, questing for El Dorado among the mountains of the moon.

The Chinese, who have venerated it always, provided the market for shang at the time our country was born. In 1784, the *Empress of China* set sail from New York for

Canton with a cargo made up entirely of wild ginseng. The Chinese received the shipment and clamored for more, even though ginseng had been cultivated in their own country for more than two millennia. It has ever been their most important drug, a plant of power and the essence of the perfect yin. They believe it gives energy to the body, acts to cure diseases, and that it delays the aging process. It is also much used as an aphrodisiac.

The shape of the root is fantastic. It twists and gnarls itself into a multitude of forms, which sometimes resemble a man. That particular root is especially valued by the Chinese, and if the man-form shows an appendage between the "legs," they sell it exclusively as a sexual stimulant.

Above ground, the plant is easily spotted. This is especially true in the late fall when its leaves, turned bright yellow and topped by a single cluster of crimson berries, shine through their drab surroundings like fabulous Yule ornaments. Thus, the plant is usually searched for in autumn, but there is no season for shanging. You may dig out the root anytime.

I prefer to search in early spring because of certain advantages. First, it's too soon for mosquitoes, those vile insects that have caused immeasurable misery to outdoorsmen. Also, there's no shooting season and I have the woods to myself. But the primary benefit is that the rattlesnakes continue to hibernate. I have a very healthy respect for these hillside rattlesnakes. They are usually huge and always dangerous and they love to coil themselves within a patch of ginseng. The common belief is that a healthy man will not expire from a rattlesnake bite. I hope those who espouse this philosophy are correct, but I would not like to lie alone on a hillside with two poisoned punctures in my arm, waiting to find out.

Granted, the ginseng plant is not as easily seen in the spring. Its leaves are not vivid and the berries are pale instead of scarlet, but I accept these minor impediments and I exult in the absence of rattlesnakes.

Ginseng has become so sparse that one can wander among the hills day after day and not see one plant, never glimpse the clustered berries. But if you hold a love of nature and stop to look about, you may see other things. Perhaps a young doe, ghosting between the hills and followed by an antlered buck, both utterly silent in their twilight trek across a draw. Or a flock of wild turkeys, gliding down a sloping hill with great outspread wings supporting their heavy bodies. They come with a rush and sweep by on a rustle of air. Or you might look up to a mass of crimson, frost-stung leaves, or feel the cool wind wash over you, laden with the odor of muscadine grapes. These are incidental discoveries to be enjoyed, but to find that which is sought affords the greatest pleasure.

It's still possible to sight those lustrous leaves of shang. On rare occasions, I've even discovered a small patch of half a dozen plants or more. Harvesting them is an easy matter. Just dig around the roots with a garden spade and pluck them from the earth. Separate them from the plant itself, brush away the dirt, and place them in a bag. At home, they must be washed and spread out in the sun to dry. If there is no sun, you may place them in an oven, but the sun is better. An experienced gatherer will know when his shang is ready for market. He can tell by the color and the weight and the taste. If he has hoarded his roots for a while, the sale may amount to several thousand dollars, especially if there are man-forms among the crop.

An assemblage of ginseng roots, laid out in the sun, presents a plethora of images. Tiny men, of course, but also clusters of snakes and misshapen animals and anything else the mind is capable of conjuring. Smell the root and there's a tangy spice in your nostrils, taste it and you will experience the perfect blend of bitter and sweet.

I have sought this elusive plant in all weathers and seasons, from my youth into old age, and have found much pleasure in the seeking. As a child, I hunted with my friends, and we were a noisy, capricious bunch. We called ourselves the "Shang Tong." Our group was formed as a covert organization, which mainly hunted ginseng, but which also met to plan clandestine adventures. We used a secret sign. I cannot fully describe this signal for fear of compromising other members, but it involved a certain digging motion with the hands.

We generally found the shang on the eastern side of our hills and believed that it grew there because, to our childish minds, that side was closer to the Orient. And this was part of the drama that ginseng held for us. We didn't reason that it was there because the east side was better protected against prevailing weather, just as it didn't occur to us that insects bored into the root because of its softness. We believed the bugs gathered because of the root's magical attraction, its power to make every living creature seek it out.

Now, the Shang Tong is no more and all its members are man-forms. And soon the wild ginseng will no longer grow on the hillsides. It is gradually fading from view and from our collective memory.

But somewhere in the interior of those Arkansas hills, an untouched field of ginseng may remain, a virgin expanse of waving leaves and glistening berries, a gold mine of man-shaped roots. I envisage it in my dreams, and I see myself out in the middle of it, spade in hand, digging up my treasure.

And in that faraway field, there are no rattlesnakes.

The Tom

It is just past daybreak and the rain falls straight down through the forest. Fat drops splash on the tree limbs and beat against the new leaves. The sound of the rainfall drums in my ears. Yesterday, the weather was different: bright sunshine lighting up a cloudless sky and no hint of the rain to come. I had driven out in my pickup truck on the day before turkey season to scout a flock I'd been watching for three days. It included three hens, three jakes, young males, and one lone tom who clearly ruled the group. Each day they had fed in a wheat field, now laying off to my right, and in the evening they'd returned to roost in an immense oak tree, growing about a hundred yards to my front.

I can't see the tree, but I know they are there now. They are waiting for the rain to stop so they can return to the field and feed in the wheat and spread their wet feathers to the sun. I will wait, too. It is only an April shower. Soon it will stop and the turkeys will come to the field and I'll call the old tom to me.

He is a massive bird. The other turkeys are fully grown, but their leader towers over them and seems twice as broad. I believe he will go at least thirty pounds. I want him badly. I have thought about him for three days.

I huddle beneath a spreading hickory and pull the collar of my camouflage coveralls tighter around my neck. My twelve gauge Remington is getting wet, but that doesn't matter. It will later be dried and oiled with no harm done. What concerns me is my turkey call. I fish it from a front pocket and make sure that it's secure in the plastic cover. Once wet, the wood may warp and it will become useless. This rectangle of cedar, known as a "box call," is composed of a hollow box, topped by a paddle. A screw at one end of the paddle secures it to the box, which acts as a sounding board. The free part of the wooden paddle is stroked against the sharp edges of the sounding board and the "yelp" of a turkey hen is produced. With a bit of practice, most hunters can adequately imitate this soft, seductive call, irresistible to a gobbler on the make.

A change has occurred in the forest. I sense the difference and then I realize what it is. The thrumming of the rain has lessened. Finally, only a slow dripping can be heard. The morning grows brighter, giving depth and definition to the surrounding woods. I peer to my right and try to locate the wheat field. I can just see it through the trees. As I look back to the left, a swath of sunlight lays itself across the treetops. The day has come with a rush and I get stiffly to my feet. I see the wheat field plainly, despite all the intervening growth, and I head toward it. The wheat leaves glimmer in the light.

In my mind's eye I trace what has already happened. The turkeys awakened a few moments ago and sat rain-soaked and sodden on the oak limbs. Then, the morning light touched them and they spread their great wings, gliding down from the treetop. Led by the tom, they headed for the wheat field. They are there now, I know, ruffling and drying their feathers in the sun.

I reach the edge of the forest and look out. The field is barren of turkeys. Only the new wheat stretches away in a emerald expanse. I retreat back into the woods and decide to get nearer the roosting place. I estimate the oak tree to be about a hundred yards away. I'll go fifty yards, keeping the wheat field in sight. I don't dare approach any nearer. The turkeys would spot me and fly off into the deeper woods and no amount of calling would retrieve them. Before starting, I bring the double-barreled shotgun up and break open the breach. A three-inch Magnum shell, filled with six shot, rests in each chamber. I snap the breach closed and gaze fondly at the weapon. Its twin twenty-six inch long barrels are both fully choked, which means they are constructed to hold the discharged pellets in a tight pattern. It is beautifully made and capable of great range and power. It's what I must have for the tom I seek.

The forest floor is wet and spongy, enabling me to move quietly toward the oak tree. I keep looking to my right, but the field remains empty. Then, movement catches my eye and I snap my head to the front. The turkeys are flying low between the tree trunks, descending toward the wheat field. Their wide wings beat up and down and the black forms seem impossibly huge as they settle to the forest floor. They remain within the woods, a few yards from the edge of the field. I kneel on the ground and wait.

Time passes slowly and there is no sound or movement. I'm undecided what to do. If they're heading back into the woods I should start calling now. If they're going into the wheat field I need to stay where I am and keep quiet. It will be easier to call the tom to me if he's in the field. He'll be more quickly drawn from the sunlit spaces into the dark and inviting woods, the secret woods, where a waiting hen cries out her soft entreaty. I decide to stay silent. For three days they have gone from the oak tree to the field. They will go there again.

"GOODOOLOODOOLOODLE!"

The old tom's gobble vibrates in the air and all seven birds step away from the woods and into the wheat field. They move in a straight line toward the center of the field, and then, following the tom's lead, they head back to the right. Presently, the whole flock is feeding in an area just opposite me. I watch them move forward and dart their heads into the foot high wheat. They are eating the young grasshoppers. The tom sounds off again and is answered by faint yelps from his flock. The sun has dried their feathers and lifted their spirits. The leader stands apart and suddenly swells and fluffs himself. His tail spreads in a great fan and the wings push downward and touch the ground. He begins to strut and his "beard", a tuft of feathers hanging from his breast, swings back and forth.

I stare at him a moment and then take the cedar paddle on my call box and scrape it once against the base. The sound that comes forth is something between a yelp and a chirp. I have given much practice to my call box and the sound it makes is the right one. It is the cry of a lonesome hen.

The tom looks in my direction and answers with a

gobble. I reply and he gobbles again and heads toward me. The rest of the flock go about their feeding, but the gobbler keeps coming. I continue with a steady series of calls until he reaches the woods and enters them. I can no longer see him, but he gobbles twice more and I answer each time. The tom does not respond to my final call. Silence surrounds us, broken only by the distant tapping of a woodpecker. I decide not to call again and remain kneeling on the ground. The pervasive quiet lengthens. I continue to wait.

Suddenly, to my front, a line of brush shakes and heaves, and the great bird bursts through it, heading toward me at a run. He is puffed again and his paintbrush beard drags the ground. Halfway across the small clearing, he sees me and comes to a shuddering stop. My gun is already to my shoulder and I sight along the barrels at the pale head. His round eyes stare back at me. They are filled with astonishment.

The right muzzle of the Remington erupts and my tom is flopping on the ground, his enormous wings hammering furiously. They cease beating as I move toward him. The other turkeys have heard the shot and are flying away from me. They rise and bank toward the left, back into the treetops.

Tonight, one of the jakes will take the old tom's place.

I bend over him and grasp the two feet. I heft him from the forest floor and stagger with the weight. There is plenty of food here and I am swept by a great sense of achievement. It took knowledge and skill and a hunter's instinct to bring the old tom down.

But even in this moment, a nagging little voice is speaking within me. It is soft and insistent and it cannot be denied because it speaks to a guilty conscience.

He was proud and magnificent, the little voice says, *and you took advantage of him. He came looking for love and renewal of life. He found you waiting instead.*

The little voice finally fades away, but the sense of achievement remains. I lift the tom to my shoulder and head back toward my truck.

The Dangerous Relative

Crowley's Ridge runs along the eastern edge of Arkansas, ending at Helena, its southernmost point. Small farms nestle on either side of the Ridge and they are host to a variety of domesticated animals. Cattle graze in the pastures, chickens wander about the front yards, and hogs wallow tranquilly in their pens. They are all meat providers, although eggs may be the only thing asked from the hens and just milk required from the cows. The pigs, however, are there for one sole purpose and that is to furnish their owners with an assortment of chops, bacon, sausage, and ham. For this, they are well suited since they gain weight quickly, will eat almost anything, and are very docile and easy to manage. They seem quite content to lie in their muddy pens, gobble from the hog trough, and happily turn themselves into pork. Watching them squeal and waddle about, it's hard to conceive that in the hills above them dwells a dangerous relative, a wild cousin, about as similar to them in appearance and temperament as a wolf is to a lap dog.

They are called *Razorbacks* or *Tush Hogs* and they have long roamed the hills and gorges of Crowley's Ridge. In the beginning they were domestic swine that had wandered into the hills and remained there, becoming feral things, foraging and breeding in the wilderness. After a few generations, the offspring looked nothing like their forebears. These creatures were totally wild with long snouts and sharp, pointed tusks, which they used like sabers to slash at their victims. Always aggressive, they would attack almost anything that moved. Now, the Razorbacks are few in number and seldom seen, but people who occasionally come upon them will always remember the meeting.

Luke Hammond, owner of a hillside farm, encountered one once and thereby lost Rube, his favorite dog. One of Luke's cows had wandered off and he and the dog went into the hills to look for it. Their search had been in vain and they were plodding down a draw, which led back to Luke's house. The sun had sunk below the treetops and filled the forest with shadowy dimness. Suddenly, to the right of them, a stand of mulberry bushes began to violently shake. The shaking stopped, and immediately afterward they heard a large animal lunging away. Rube gave a low growl and charged after it. He was a big, powerful dog and he split straight through the quivering bushes. Luke heard another growl, followed by a short yelp. Running toward the sound, he also crashed through the bushes. What he saw on the other side brought him to a sliding halt. The savage sow had already killed the dog. Rube was a crumpled heap of fur. The hog stood over him and she was staring at Luke. The blood dripping from her tusks appeared quite dark in the fading light. Luke remained stock-still and the Tush Hog took a few steps toward him. Then, she turned and disappeared into the undergrowth. Luke gathered up his cattle dog and carried him home.

I am another who once met a Razorback. I came upon him, as Luke did, in the fading light of day, but I had no dog to give him and he came for me instead.

When walking in the hills, it's easier to travel along the ridge tops. They are generally free of obstruction and sometimes offer paths. On this late October afternoon, I was returning home from squirrel hunting with three of the "bushytails" tucked into the rear of my hunting vest. Their comfortable weight had me thinking on how my wife should prepare them for supper. Lightly breaded and fried to a crispy brown, that seemed the proper course. And naturally with gravy and hot biscuits.

My mind gradually left the supper table and returned to my surroundings. Rain laden clouds hung just above the forest and veils of mist drifted between the tree trunks. The gorges below the ridge were already filled with darkness, and gorge and ridge alike lay blanketed in silence. I was treading a descending path over soaked leaves and my steps did not disturb the stillness so the explosive snort from below came with startling clarity. I halted and peered down into the shadows and heard another snorting grunt. This was followed by the thrumming of quick, hoofed feet. That sound grew louder as I listened. Something was rushing up out of the gloom.

The huge boar broke through a patch of blackberry vines and stepped onto the path in front of me. He stood staring down the other side of the hill and I had a moment to observe the hard, rangy body, the massive head. Dingy tusks jutted out and upward from his long snout, ending in sharp points just above the nostrils.

It is said that the Razorback is the only wild animal on the North American continent that will attack a man without provocation, that this attack is always instant and automatic. I decided to take no chances and very slowly raised the shotgun toward my shoulder. That was all it took. The boar sensed the movement and whirled to face me. His red, piggish eyes bored into me and he made a slashing movement with his head.   An instant later, he had lowered that head and was charging toward me.

I snapped the gun butt to my shoulder, sighted briefly at the oncoming beast, and squeezed the trigger. A sharp click sounded in my ears and my heart dropped. I had not reloaded the shotgun. The boar was almost upon me when I hurled the weapon at him. It hit the ground between us and the Razorback came to a stop. He lifted his head and regarded me for a long moment. Had he not been an animal, I would have read it as a look of contempt. I slowly backed away, planting my feet carefully behind me and watching him all the while. Once again, he slashed the air with those murderous tusks and then he wheeled and trotted down the hill.

But just before entering the shadows, the boar stopped once more and turned completely around to face me. We stood there for a long moment, looking at each other. I do not recollect his turning away a final time. Rather, he seemed to waver, losing shape and substance and gradually fading into his surroundings, absorbed at last into the woods and a world of unknowable wildness.

I retrieved my gun, making sure to re-load this time, and hurried along the narrow path. I was anxious to escape the forest before darkness finally caught me. Eventually, I reached the edge of the woods and stepped out onto a grassy and at once familiar slope. Near the bottom of the slope sat my cottage, smoke curling away from the chimney, windows aglow with lamplight, and my wife, standing in the doorway, her eyes searching the hills. She saw me, smiled, and lifted her arm.

I took in the view below, then turned for a last long look at what lay behind me, so different in all its aspects from anyone's hearth and home. Finally, I faced forward, returned my wife's wave, and with quickening steps, descended into a gentler world.

The Hunter

My old man was a hunter. Now, perhaps that puts a half-formed image of him in your head. But if you think he owned a collection of guns, or kept a pack of hounds, or that he spent nights in a deer camp with other men, you would be wrong. My father was a hunter on a very primitive level. He hunted only for food. To kill something that would not ultimately be eaten was foreign to him. Trophy hunting? Not within his understanding. The old man was a predator, along with the bobcat and the wolf and the hawk.

Also, except when I was with him, he hunted alone. Simple and solitary hunting, yes, but with a profound knowledge of his prey and the forest. He had mastered stealth and silence. He was always aware of the wind.

My father never sought to instruct me on a hunt, but allowed me to watch and learn. He was the best of teachers. Did he love what he did? I never knew, but I believe he got satisfaction from it, as a master will when he practices his craft.

It's Saturday morning. Yesterday, I left school behind and am resolved not to even think about it till Monday. Today, I hunt with my father. The old man had come into my room earlier to shake me awake. Now we sit at the kitchen table, drinking coffee. We are speaking softly because my mother and younger sister are still asleep. An overhead lamp sheds its glow on us and picks out white streaks in the old man's hair. He is of average height with a stringy build and weathered face. He smiles at me and wrinkles deepen around the clear, gray eyes.

"You awake yet, Bumper?" he asks.

"I'm gettin' there," I reply, and my father's smile widens.

"Well, let's get going," he says.

We stand up from the table and pluck guns from a wall rack. The old man selects a well-used Winchester 30-06 and hands me a Marlin 30-30. It is late November. We will deer hunt.

Our house on Crowley's Ridge is surrounded by miles of woods. We walk across the front yard and down a slope, covered with dead grass. Within moments, we are into the trees. My father walks ahead with a loose-kneed shamble that eats up the distance, and even with dry leaves covering the ground, makes little noise. I watch as the back of the heel comes down and the foot rolls up to the toes, effortlessly repeated. If the dead leaves weren't there, he'd make no sound at all. I have quieted my walk, but I still trudge along making enough noise for both of us. I reflect that in all our time in the woods I have never heard my father snap a twig.

We move along the top of a ridge. It is lit by early light, but the gullies on either side remain dark in their depths. Trees grow up from the darkness, but only the sunlit tops, spreading beneath our feet, are visible. The ridge is fairly free of growth and we walk along it, above the forest. A chill breeze rises to meet us and I pull my coat collar higher around my neck. My father has, of course, chosen a direction that places us downwind.

Suddenly, he stops and stares along the ridge top trail. I halt and slowly lean to the side. It would never occur to me to ask what my father sees. We seldom speak in the woods, and when we do, the words are murmured. The old man slowly stretches out his arm and I sight along it, past his fingers. A short distance ahead, the dry grass moves and I see the cane-cutter rabbit. The animal hops into the middle of the trail and sits there, twitching its long ears back and forth. The old man starts forward again and the rabbit jerks its head around. With one lengthy leap, it disappears down the hillside. My father looks behind him and I return his grin. I am happy in the old man's company. This has always been so.

Without slowing, My father strikes down the left side of the ridge and enters the thicker woods. More daylight has arrived but a dark overcast now blankets the sky. At the bottom of the hill, we turn right and the wind is once more in our faces. I perceive that we're following a faint path. The old man stops again and kneels down. I kneel behind him and immediately see the deer tracks. They are plain and plentiful, and some, even to my amateurish eye, seem recent. My father stands and looks around. Trees soar up in all directions and their barren branches crisscross overhead. A stand of mulberry bushes, surrounding an oak tree, sets off to the right. We head toward it. After entering the bushes, we both turn to face the trail and then find seats beneath the tree.

We wait.

From the old man, I have learned that hunting, especially deer hunting, is about waiting. Stalking the animal is, to say the least, unprofitable. Even the one who shares my tree, this most silent and proficient of hunters, must wait.

The morning grows warmer. My head slips forward on my chest and my eyes begin to close. I force them open and cast a guilty look at my father. The old man reaches over and pats me on the knee. After a moment, my head drops again and I begin to doze.

To my brief sleep, there comes a lucid dream. I'm standing at the end of a wooded corridor and I can see a figure approaching through that tunnel of trees. It is a hunter and he's wearing buckskin clothing. A coonskin cap sets atop his head and a flintlock rifle rests in the crook of his arm. Bushes rustle on either side and I know, without seeing them, that scores of Indians lurk there. The hunter draws closer and I see that it's my father. I try to shout. I have to warn him, but no sound comes from my throat. Then, one of the Indians steps out and stands beside the trail. Another joins him and another. More emerge from the other side until two lines of tall warriors stand along the way. My father walks between them. He removes his coonskin cap and waves it over his head and I no longer am afraid. I know why the Indians are there. They have come to see my father. They have come to pay him tribute.

Suddenly, I wake up and quickly look about me. My father has risen and slipped to the undergrowth's edge. I get to my feet and watch. He stands motionless and all seems motionless with him. Even the breeze has ceased.

Then, my father's rifle rises smoothly to his shoulder and the muzzle erupts in a shattering crash that echoes back and forth among the hills. He moves forward and vanishes and I rush to where he stood.

The young buck lies on its side in the middle of the trail and the old man crouches beside it. He rises to his feet, and the hunting knife, clasped in his right hand, drips blood on the dry leaves. I freeze in place because it seems I'm beholding a different person, a savage stranger, who looks up from his kill and regards me with fierce and predatory eyes. Then the figure grins and beckons and I see that it's just my father. I give a shout and rush forward to join him on the trail.

The Trotline

I never understood people who run trotlines. After all, the whole idea of fishing is to fish, to physically be there and fish, with you at one end of the line and your catch on the other. A trotline is a trap. You set this trap for the fish and you go away and you come back later and pick up whatever finned prisoner awaits, fishing without the fun of fishing; might as well pick'em up at the market. No, I never understood running a trotline, until I came to Old Town Lake.

Southwest of Helena, Arkansas on State Highway 20, sits the deserted settlement of Old Town. Nothing remains but a ramshackle store building, standing empty beside the road, and the rotting remains of a cotton gin. Weeds and Johnson grass have reclaimed the rest, covering the yards and gardens of a people long departed. Something like ten miles further on, you come to Old Town Lake. Huge and shallow, this body of water covers hundreds of acres of rich delta soil, acres that sank during an ancient earthquake.

Immense cypress trees ring the lake and grow well out toward its center.

These trees symbolize the lake. Nothing but cypress grows here and you cannot think of the lake without thinking of the trees. The enormous trunks rise up from the lake bed like temple columns and their offspring, the myriad "cypress knees" rear out of the water around them. They form a forest, a dark woods, with a floor, covered not with grass or leaves, but by the murky depths of Old Town Lake itself. And in those depths live the shoals of catfish, moving among the cypress knees and the great tree trunks, and feeding off the lake's rich bottom. Sometimes, they rise from their bottom feeding and seek nourishment above, perhaps a living morsel, or a scrap of food, thrown from a boat. Often their snack is attached to a line with a fisherman on the other end. And sometimes, it's secured to a trotline.

To this lake, in the fall of the year and the dying part of a day, come my two brothers and I. We have left Helena, driving out of Crowley's Ridge in an aged, rusty pickup of indeterminate color, following the two-lane blacktop of Highway 20.

In the back of the truck sets an ice chest full of ice, a cardboard box holding various grocery items, a kerosene lantern, a small folded up tent, some camping articles and fish bait, three life vests, a boat paddle, and 75 yards of fully assembled trotline, all this resting within the confines of a 12 foot metal johnboat. We sit shoulder to shoulder in the cab and watch denuded cotton fields slide by. Old Town appears on the left. Our faces turn toward it and we gaze at its ghostly passage.

Ahead, lofty cypress trees stretch along the horizon.

They are the presage of Old Town Lake. Soon, we arrive and park up-slope from a tree. Brown, dry grass covers the ground, and on the other side of the tree, the waters of the lake begin.

My youngest brother turns off the ignition and fumbles a cigarette from a pack on the dashboard. Turning toward us, he says:

"Whaddaya say we set up right here? It's a good place to put the boat in."

"Yeah, but is it a good place to string the trotline?" This from the middle brother, who's never been on Old Town Lake before.

Billy surveys the tree line and says, "Good as any, Don. We go out to where the tree line ends and find two cypress the right distance apart. Then we string the line between them. Only thing to worry about is if the water's deep enough. The catfish are everywhere."

I've been sitting on the right and I open the truck door and climb out. I stretch my arms over my head and look around. "Won't you need to tie the tent up between something?" I ask "This is the only tree around that's on dry ground."

Donald gets out on the same side and lays a hand on my shoulder. "Harold," he says in a voice thick with condescension. "You don't have to do that anymore. My tent comes with its own supports. They fit inside and make the tent stand up, sorta like a big umbrella." Then, turning toward the youngest, who's climbing out of the driver's side, "You know, our big brother needs to learn more about the great outdoors, maybe go on a field trip. He knows nothing of tents. He knows nothing of camping. This man you see before you has never run a trot line."

Grinning, Billy grinds his cigarette out on the truck

fender. "Well, you better be careful," he replies in his soft voice, "if you want him to write nice things about you."

My brothers and I walk behind the old Ford and begin unloading its cargo. We take everything but paddle and life vests out of the boat and stack them beneath the tree. Next, Billy and Don lift the boat out of the truck bed, carry it over to the lake, and slide it into the water. A rope hangs from the boat's front and Billy secures the loose end to a cypress knee.

I start sorting things out beneath the tree and my brothers turn to the tent. They have it up in a matter of moments. It even *looks* like a big umbrella. I hang our lantern from a low branch, and after looking at the lengthening shadows, decide to light it. The wick flares up and casts a yellow glow around us. Billy erects the portable grill and fills one side with charcoal. He lights it and sets coffee to boiling. Looking over at Donald, he says:

"Let's set out the trotline while there's still some daylight."

Don gives him a suspicious look and asks, "What'd you bring for bait?"

"Ripe chicken guts. They've been out in the sun for three days."

"Oh, no," says Don, taking a step backward. "First time you took me with you, we used rotten chicken guts. Second time it was rotten chicken guts and I'm the one who had to handle 'em. Well, I told you then, little brother, and I'm telling you now. No more chicken guts. There's *got* to be something else a catfish likes to eat."

"Well, there *is* something else, Don, and I brought it, knowing how squeamish you are. It's called Stink Lure. Got it at the bait shop. They say it's pretty good, but I still think chicken guts are best."

"Yeah, 'cause you always take *me* along to dig'em out," replied Don, hefting the bucket of bait.

Billy picks up the roll of trotline and he and Don get in the boat. Billy backs off from the bank. He makes a strong sideways sweep with the paddle and the little boat swings quickly around. Two more strokes and they disappear into the shadowy stand of cypress.

I walk back to check on the charcoal and coffee, then start out to look for firewood. I gather an armload of dead branches, return to the campsite, and place them in a pile. Taking an aluminum pan from the camping articles, I set it on the grill beside the coffee pot and fill it half full of vegetable oil. Looking around for something else to do, I spy the lawn chairs and arrange all three around the firewood. I don't intend to light the fire until my brothers come back.

The light fades and a chill wind springs up, rustling the thick, dead grass. Somewhere down the lake bank, a night bird sounds a lonely note. I take a seat in one of the chairs and wait for my brothers return.

After a while, I hear them, low voices murmuring in the gloom. In a moment, the bow of the boat floats into the camp light. The two clamber out and drag their craft halfway up the bank. I pour some charcoal lighter on my pile of wood and strike a match. The dry branches catch quickly and living flames writhe through them. They give off a welcomed warmth and add their flickering light to the lantern glow. The smell of burning wood blends with the aroma of coffee.

"That didn't take long," I say.

"'Course not, replies Don. "Laying trotlines is our business."

"Yeah, well, I just hope you two remember where you laid it."

Casting his gaze skyward, Don says, "This from a man who, before today, has never even seen a trotline."

Billy fishes some cups out of the box and pours coffee for us. He looks about him in his quiet way and says, "Well, at least he keeps a good campsite."

"How long do we wait before we run it," I ask him?

"Oh, we'll give it a couple of hours."

We lean back in our lawn chairs, sip the hot, black coffee, and stare into the campfire. Somewhere out in the darkness, a large fish jumps and splashes back into the water. We talk quietly and the tree frogs chime in with an occasional comment.

The fire has burned lower and we begin to feel the damp night air. Don tells us he'll get more firewood and starts down the lake bank. Billy stands up, stretches, and turns to me.

"Well, bro, wanna go take a look?"

I nod and lean forward to poke the coals a bit. Billy gets in the rear of the boat and I shove us off the bank. We turn around and head into the darkness. I flip my headlight on and the beam reaches out between the trees. Billy's paddle makes a soft, gurgling sound in the water, and cypress trunks, glistening in the light, glide slowly by. Off to our right, a bullfrog croaks and kerplunks into the still water. On an impulse, I switch off my headlight and we are immersed in darkness. A scent of live fish and decaying vegetation drifts up to me.

"Can you smell the fish," I ask?

"Can't smell a thing," my brother replies. "Can't see a thing, either. You want to turn the light back on?"

"Let there be light," I pronounce, and flip on the switch.

A tree trunk looms right in front of us and Billy swerves to miss it.

"Stop fooling around," he murmurs.

Looking forward, I notice there are less trees and more open water. My headlight beam catches a bright object. It's a piece of cloth, tied to a cypress knee. The end of our trotline is secured beneath it and descends from there into the water. I swing the light further along and notice several large "floats" lined up and disappearing into the darkness. They're spaced about ten yards apart and are used, I realize, to keep the trotline hooks suspended at an even depth. I stare at the motionless floats, resting on the lake's flat surface.

Then, without warning, one of the further ones sinks into the water. The other floats bobble, and the visible line, running from the cypress knee, yaws slowly back and forth. I turn to look at Billy and he nods his head. "Grab hold of the line," he says.

I feel the line tremble between my fingers and I instinctively lift it from the water and draw it toward me. Billy swings the end of the boat around and hand over hand I pull us toward the first float. A vertical string appears and I lift the trotline higher. The string drops about three feet and a ball of bait, the "Stink Lure", covers a hook at the end of it. The bait feels soft and is the color of old blood. It smells like something old blood would ooze from.

"Bait still on," Billy asks?

I tell him that it is and pull past the float to the next hook. It rises, naked and gleaming, and I fish around for the bait bucket. I take one of the smelly balls out, look at it, and decide to use two of them. I mold both around the hook and let it drop into the water.

"Uh-huh," comes the approving voice behind me.

The line lunges again as I take it in my hand. "Shouldn't we go ahead and get that fish off?" I ask.

Billy chuckles. "Amateurs head straight for the fish. Us professionals bait the hooks as we go. I think he's on the next hook, anyway."

He's right. The float in front of me dives under the water again and stays there. I come to it, locate the vertical string, and haul it upward.

The wide head of the catfish breaks the surface and the body follows, water flying as it twists and jerks beneath my hands. I bring it over into the boat and it lies there, smooth and glistening. Long feelers on either side of its mouth twitch back and forth. I place my right foot on the fish and remove the hook. Following Billy's instructions, I take a hammer from the tackle box and strike the head a sharp blow, just between the wide-spaced eyes. The catfish stiffens, quivers a couple of times, and lies still.

"He must go at least ten pounds," exclaims Billy.

I nod my head and re-bait the hook. We finish running the line and head back toward the bank. I can see our campfire glimmering through the trees.

Donald eyes the fish as we come up and goes over to put charcoal under the vegetable oil. Billy strings the catfish up by its head and skins it, using a knife to slice the skin, and pliers to pull it off in long strips. After dressing the fish, he takes the filets down to the lake and washes them. Not long after, they float breaded and sizzling in the boiling oil. Hushpuppies, prepared beforehand, also go into the oil, and soon the smell of fresh fried fish and spicy cornmeal have us rummaging for our dinner plates.

* * *

The night has grown older and we have settled into silence. Our stomachs are full and we sit dozing in our camp chairs. Presently, Don and Billy leave to run the trotline again. Three sleeping bags lay spread out behind me. I walk over to mine, take off my shoes, and slide into it. Lying on my back, I can hear a late wind rustling through the cypress boughs and lake water lapping against the bank and I can hear my brothers voices dwindling away, carried away across the surface of Old Town Lake.

And I remember that it was at this precise moment I came to understand why people run trotlines.

Jump

In the beginning a bullfrog is a fish, hatched from an egg like any other fish, and swimming in the depths of a pond. He possesses gills instead of lungs, has a streamlined legless body, and he never rises to the surface. He is a fish.

Then changes start to occur. His gills turn into lungs, four legs sprout from his body, and the fish-like shape disappears. Eventually, he hops out onto the bank, and lo, he is a bullfrog. Also, he is an amphibian, which means he can still live under the water as well as on dry land. That's only one of his remarkable characteristics.

The bullfrog never takes a drink of water. He absorbs it through his skin, and he breathes that way as well. He also breathes with his lungs and through the roof of his mouth. Any one of these methods will keep the bullfrog alive. And his tongue is attached to the front of his mouth rather than the back. It is very sticky and he flips the entire length of it out to catch flying insects. The remainder of his diet consists of small birds and other frogs.

Other frogs? Small birds? Yes, our bullfrog is a pretty big frog. As a matter of fact, he's the largest frog in North America and can grow to more than a foot in length. His long, muscular legs account for more than half this span, and with them the bullfrog can leap prodigious distances. He uses them to jump away from danger. The bullfrog jumps to live. And therein lies a paradox, because the legs that so often save the bullfrog's life may eventually cause his early demise, the reason being that frog legs taste delicious.

Hold one of these deep-fried, golden morsels between thumb and forefinger, let your teeth break through the thin, crispy crust and sink into the tasty flesh and you will quickly see that this is so. And you may feel compelled to join me as a fellow hunter of bullfrogs, since one sure way of obtaining frog legs is to go out and get the frog.

Hornor's Nook, a small lake lying east of Crowley's Ridge, is situated between that ridge of hills and the great Mississippi River. Oak and hickory trees surround the lake, casting green reflections in the springtime and shimmering orange and yellows in the fall. The edges of the Nook are shallow, with vegetation growing along the bottom. And they are home to a thousand bullfrogs.

Frogging is done after dark, and on a soft spring night, strewn with patches of fog, my brother and I come to this place in search of our supper. We unload a ten-foot johnboat from the back of my pickup and lower it into the water. A small electric trolling motor is attached to the stern. I shine my waterproof MagLite into the boat and check its contents. A 12 volt battery sets next to the motor and is attached to it with electric cables. The boat also contains a paddle, two life preservers, a cloth bag, and a frog gig. This last item is comprised of a long wooden handle, capped by a metal trident. The three prongs are short, slender, and quite close together. A miniature barb protrudes from just behind each needle like point. It is clearly a weapon.

We get into the boat and I shove us away from the bank. I flip a button on the trolling motor handle and we glide silently across the water. My brother perches in the bow. He has lifted the gig, and being a southpaw, holds it poised in his left hand. I can barely see him. It is a moonless night and we are immersed in darkness. I have not yet switched on the flashlight. I turn right and start moving parallel with the bank. Suddenly the silence is broken by a single course, grunting croak. Further along the bank, an answering "Ruuurruump" is heard. Other voices join in, and in a moment, the night is filled with the calling of bullfrogs.

I finally switch on my flashlight and aim it toward the bank. I search for areas that are free of growth. It would be pointless to look elsewhere. There must always be a passage for the boat. The flashlight beam travels as the boat travels. It moves across a bare stretch of clay bank and I see two tiny lights gleaming back at me. They are close together and give off a silvery shine, and, of course, they are not lights at all. They are the reflecting eyes of a bullfrog. My brother sees them also and looks back at me. I nod and turn toward the bank, reducing our speed as we go.

We have coasted close to the bank and I can see our quarry quite clearly. He seems immense. The eyes have lost their shine, but his moist skin glistens in the light. We draw closer and my brother slowly brings the gig downward until its prongs are pointing at the frog. He reposes on the bank like some squatting idol. His powerful hind legs are tucked beneath him and he remains completely still, staring into the light. It is the light that holds him so. He is mesmerized by it. If the light remains on him and he sees or hears or feels nothing, he will remain motionless.

We are only a few feet away.

Now is the time for silence and patience and stealth. If he hears a gurgle of water from the boat, he will jump. If he feels the slightest tremor beneath his fat belly, he will jump. If the flashlight beam wavers for an instant against his protruding eyes, he will jump.

The boat drifts in slowly.

My brother places both hands on the gig handle, about midway down its length. He leans forward and freezes in place, his eyes fixed on our prey. The prong's points are a yard from the frog's body. I hold the flashlight beam rock steady on him, and when the barbed points are less than a foot away, my brother shoots them forward.

Instantly, the frog begins to rise, and in my mind's eye, I can see the jump, see him sailing past the boat, moving upward and outward and kerplunking into the lake.

But he has lingered in the light beam an instant too long and the jump was only a thought in his froggish brain. The middle point catches him in the back, driving all the way through, and pinning him to the lake bank.

Don pulls him into the boat and plucks him from the prong. Taking a clasp knife from his pocket, he opens a small blade and pierces the bullfrog's head. The creature quivers once and grows still. My brother places him in the bag and dips it into the water. This will keep him moist and fresh.

We continue along the lake bank and gather eleven more frogs. Only one eludes us and this was a disappointment because he was larger than the others. However, the boat bumped a branch on the way in and that was all it took. Our quarry leapt a good twelve feet before splashing into the water.

I heft the bulging sack as we head back toward the pickup. Twenty-four frog legs will make a nice meal. I can picture them freshly fried, crusty brown, and served with corn meal muffins.

The air is tremulous with the sound of bullfrogs.

I'm thinking of the huge frog that got away and I remember how he looked, soaring past our heads, his long legs stretched behind him. I know that when the waters enclosed him, he folded those legs beneath his great body and sank down through the currents, sank gently down until he finally came to rest on the bottom of Hornor's Nook.

He sits there now and he is utterly motionless. He does not even need to breathe. The waters, bearing its life giving oxygen, seeps in through his skin and permeates his body and makes him one with the lake. He will rest and ponder for a while, and then his powerful legs will thrust him back to the surface.

Perhaps, on another spring night, my light will once more find him on the lake bank. I will hold him steady in my beam and we will draw closer and closer to each other. For a brief moment, we will be very close, and then I'll catch him on my gig.

Or he will jump, saving himself in the way that nature provided, ascending on those marvelous legs to plunge, once again, into the sanctum of the nook.

The Trapper

My friend, the trapper, lives on a wooded hill. A line of adjoining hills stretch northward toward Missouri and this piece of country is known as Crowley's Ridge. The trapper has lived here all his life and has depended on the Ridge for a large part of his livelihood. He has used its trees to build his simple cabin and plowed its soil for his annual garden. The forest around him has never failed to supply fresh meat in the form of deer and squirrels and rabbits. He hunts them only in their season and as he needs them. The trapper works at odd jobs in the nearby town of Medford, and to supplement his income, he runs a trap line.

This is the trapper talking to me over a cup of coffee in the Elite Café:

"I started running traps when I was ten years old. 'Course, I didn't run 'em alone. My daddy was with me. He's the one taught me how. They was his traps and it was his trap line. It wasn't till I growed up that I run my own line. That was sixty years ago. Things was different then. The Ridge was full of mink and a good trapper could make some money at it. Now, they're awful scarce, but I'll still catch a mink now and then."

I have asked for this meeting and it's time to make my request. "Are you running your traps tomorrow?"

"Sure," he answers, "run 'em every day till the season ends."

"Would you mind if I came along with you?"

The old man cocks an eye at me and says, "Trap lines are run early, right at first light."

"I'll be there," I say.

The trapper looks out the restaurant window. Early darkness has crept in and the street lights glimmer through a frosty mist. Heavy flakes of snow sweep past the window. "We'll be getting some more of that stuff," he says. "Better dress for it."

Next morning, we're drinking coffee at the old man's kitchen table, and after a long drive through darkness, I'm struggling to stay awake. We empty our cups and my companion rinses them in the sink. We're both wearing insulated boots, thick pants, and woolen shirts. We put on our heavy hunting coats and step outside.

The old man's house sets on a ridge, running east and west, and we walk away westward. The sky behind has lightened just enough for us to see our way. A thin covering of frozen snow lays over our path and crunches beneath our feet. The wind is blowing. It's not a strong wind, but it is steady. It sweeps out of the west and up the sloping ridge and numbs our cheeks and noses. I reach into my pockets and bring out my gloves.

The trapper is walking in front. Suddenly, he leaves the trail and heads down the left slope. I follow along. At the bottom is a shallow pond, and next to it, a fallen tree. Its roots are tangled around each other like a bulbous nest of snakes. The trapper points to a certain spot and I can see that a pathway has been made through the roots and dead grass. He kneels, brushes twigs and snow aside, and the wide-open jaws of a trap appear. They are connected to a pair of leaf springs. At the center of the jaws is a round metal disk. I can see how the trap works. When the disk is pressed down, the jaws snap shut. A thin chain secures the trap to a nearby root. The old man carefully covers the trap with more forest debris and we move on, following the edge of the pond.

My companion does not need to point out the next trap. A splashing sound comes from just ahead of us and I can see a small bush, violently shaking. I can also see an animal beneath it, standing belly deep in the water. The creature is squirming frantically, twisting this way and that, trying to escape. As we approach, it stops and stares at us with little red eyes. Its delicate, oval-shaped head is attached to a long, sinuous body, ending in a tapered tail. It is a mink. The left rear foot is caught in the trap. It gives a final yank with that foot and then stands quietly, watching the trapper approach. My companion jerks a wooden club from his belt and gives the animal a sharp whack across the back of the head. It shudders once and grows still. The trapper then opens the jaws of the trap and lifts the mink free. He stuffs it into the back of his hunting coat and resets the trap. As we continue along, he begins to talk:

"Fifty years ago, these hills was full of mink, but they was also full of poor folk. And, because mink pelts brought a good price, they was finally trapped out and just about *wiped* out. Now, the big mink breeding farms furnish all the pelts. The mink on Crowley's Ridge are still scarce. During the season, I might gather one or two a week, and at $30.00 a hide, that ain't much."

The trapper walks on with his purposeful tread and I know it would never occur to him that what he's doing might be brutal or cruel. To him, it is a harvesting of skins.

We come to the end of the trap line and I watch my companion replace brush and leaves over the final (and empty) trap. The others have also been empty. We head back toward his cabin. The trapper's stride has not slowed since we began and he shows no sign of fatigue. My breath has shortened and I must struggle to keep up. This I'm determined to do because I'm not about to let a seventy year old man walk off and leave me.

My watch tells me it's mid-morning, but the thick treetops and low clouds darken and diffuse the light. Huge, drifting snowflakes begin to fill the air. They float down thicker and faster and become curtains of snow, sweeping back and forth among the tree trunks. Finally, the old man's cabin comes into view and he invites me inside.

We sit at his kitchen table and drink the hot, strong coffee. I can feel each swallow warming me all the way to my stomach. The trapper empties his cup and says:

"Well, I'd better skin him before he gets stiff."

He hauls the mink from his coat and we walk out onto the front porch. I hold the mink's hind legs while the trapper, with a few deft cutting and pulling motions, separates the animal from its fur. The old man takes the carcass, flings it into the woods, and murmurs, "Food for the critters." He then takes a wooden frame and stretches the hide over it, skin outward.

"It'll need to dry for a few days," he says.

I thrust my hand into the fur. It is luxuriant and soft and the color of dark honey. My mind flies away and I imagine it in its future place as part of some rich woman's coat. Perhaps she'll wear it to a dinner party, given by the best people, and they'll all gather round her.

"It's exquisite," some matron will exclaim. "Wherever did it come from?"

"From Bergdorf's," she'll reply. "It's frightfully expensive, but you know, we only live once."

And the woman, wealthy and admired, will be partially correct. It *is* very expensive and we *all* only live once. But the coat did not come from Bergdorf's. Almost all of it came from the cages of a Montana mink ranch. And a small portion came from a snowy hillside, lying just west of a trapper's cabin on Crowley's Ridge.

The Deer Stand

I've got a deer stand on Crowley's Ridge, near a grove of hickory and just off a narrow trail that leads away from the hickory trees and down the hill and across a level draw. It's about the best deer stand I ever set up. It's high up in the forks of an ancient oak and hard to see from the ground. There's good open fields of fire all along the trail and just an unbelievable amount of deer sign, track upon track in the soft ground and rubbings on almost every tree in sight. I've used this deer stand once, but never got a chance to sight a buck. I don't imagine I'll ever use it again.

I set it up in late October, after trekking the Ridge all afternoon in search of a suitable site. The location, as I've mentioned, is well nigh perfect, and when I saw it, the first thing I did was look around for another deer stand. I just couldn't believe this place was overlooked, but the surrounding trees held nothing but leaves and limbs, acorns and hickory nuts. I tied a rope to my stand, climbed that oak, and pulled the stand up behind me. I had it secured in no time and was back to my hilltop cabin just after nightfall. I trudged up the hill with my eyes on our cottage, the front windows all aglow with lamp light. This was our summer retreat, and a week away from everything during deer season. A dark silhouette appeared at one of the windows. My wife, Naomi, stood staring down the trail, waiting for me to come home.

"Did you locate a place for it?" she asked, as she opened the door for me..

"You better believe it. Naomi, the place is perfect. I just hope another hunter doesn't find it."

"I didn't think that was allowed. I mean, if they see another stand they won't put theirs up, right?"

"That's pretty much the rule, but mine is real high and well concealed. They may not see it.

Naomi turned back to stove and said, "Well, don't worry about it. I don't think anyone will be going out there tonight."

"Good point," I said, grinning at her. "What's for supper?"

"Fried chicken, biscuits, and cream potatoes with gravy."

She didn't have to tell me, because I could smell it before I opened the door. I could also smell the apple pie, but I asked anyway. "And dessert?"

Naomi smiled, lowered her chin, and gave me a leering look. I was only slightly surprised. One thing I'd learned early about my normally quiet and low-key wife. When she was ready for sex, she'd let you know it, and she wanted it without much delay.

I remember how beautiful Naomi looked that night with those emerald eyes and that bountiful, red-gold hair falling past her shoulders. After the apple pie, I followed her into the bedroom and watched her step out of her shoes and remove the short, yellow sundress. Another surprise! She had nothing on underneath. This wasn't the usual Naomi, but I wasn't complaining. When she turned to face me, a seductive smile on her face, I took in the whole of her, the combination of color. Golden hair, green eyes, ivory skin, and just to counterpoint it all, a diamond-shaped, strawberry birthmark, right next to the pubic bulge. I shed my clothing and we both slipped under the bed covers.

I would never utter a course word to anyone about my wife, but this morning I sat in my tree stand and allowed my secret mind to fill with bawdy images of Naomi. What a night! What a woman! And what was that noise, coming up the trail?

For years, I had carried a Marlin .30/.30 on deer hunts. It first belonged to my daddy and it bore the scratches and scrapes of hard use. But I'd taken real good care of this rifle and wouldn't think of using anything else on a deer stand. It didn't generate much velocity and hadn't a lot of knockdown power, but it was dead on accurate at up to 300 yards and that lever action clicked in smooth as a Swiss watch. Now, I lifted it and sighted along the short barrel down the deer trail. I didn't really expect to see a buck, because what I'd heard was leaves crunching and my quarry would never ever make a sound like that. As a matter of fact, it wouldn't usually make any sound at all. I figured it for human and when I heard the sound of voices, I knew I was right. Damn nitwits! What in the world were they doing out here carrying on a conversation? My daddy used to say that only fools and jackasses brayed in the woods, and when these two jackasses came into view,

I knew right away who they were: Jim Oliphant and Cecil Jackson from back in Medford. They both wore camouflaged clothing, which included a hunting vest, and each one carried a rifle. Cecil Jackson fumbled in his vest and came out with a pint of Wild Turkey. He offered the bottle to Oliphant, but Oliphant shook his head and produced a bottle of his own. It looked like both bottles had seen some use and I figured that was the reason for this untimely chatter. They came up to my tree, jabbering away, and not even bothering to look around them. My first reaction was just plain old anger. Why in hell did these clowns have to stumble down this particular trail and onto this perfect ground. There was no way a buck would venture through here now, and by the time these two left it might be too late in the day to sight one. The next feeling to come was alarm, what if they looked up and saw me? The last thing in the world I wanted was to be forced into the company of these yahoos, or even have to speak to them. They were typical of a lot of hunters nowadays. They weren't serious about shooting game, and if truth be known, probably hoped they wouldn't see any. The only thing they really cared about was drinking whiskey and swapping lies. Usually, you found people like that laid up in a hunting lodge somewhere, swilling bourbon while everyone else was out in the woods. It was just my bad luck that these two were slightly more adventurous. And now I remembered actually being cooped up with Oliphant one night at the Crowley's Ridge Hunting Lodge. He'd spent a couple of hours bending everyone's ears about the ten pointers he'd slain and the women he'd laid. I don't know which were the bigger lies, but I seriously believe some of my buddies were about to draw straws to see who would shoot him in the morning.

So here I was, looking down at these guys and hoping they'd keep moving. I hunched closer to the tree trunk and sat still as stone. I probably didn't need to worry that much, because I was really high up, and a huge limb grew out directly between me and the ground. As a matter of fact, the two intruders were temporarily shielded from my view. However, I could here there voices plain enough. And the first thing I heard brought a chill to my liver.

"Hey Jim," said Cecil Jackson, "let's take a rest."

They moved to an opening in the leaves and I saw Jackson place his rifle against the tree trunk. He sat down and crossed his legs and then Oliphant came into view and sat down beside them. Both men leaned back and Cecil lit up a cigarette.

Well, that settled it. If all the noise and yammering didn't cause the deer to vamoose, that tobacco smoke sure would. A buck could scent that stuff for miles. Damn these morons anyway. The only thing that kept me from shinnying down the tree and cussing them out was the fact I probably wouldn't be able to get rid of them afterward. Stay still, I thought. They'll be gone soon and you can climb down and go home, or find another place for your deer stand. The smoke from the cigarette drifted upward through the branches and Cecil Jackson's voice floated up with it.

"You know what, Jim? This would be a great spot for a deer stand."

So you finally noticed, I thought. What an idiot! Back in Medford, Cecil owned a small engine shop and made his living working on lawn mowers, garden tillers, and outboard motors. Today was the first time in memory that I'd seen him without his work clothes, which consisted of a greasy pair of tan coveralls and a dirty striped cap. His partner worked for Medford Utilities and spent his days reading gas meters. It came to me that many of the meter reader's tales of seduction were about dissatisfied housewives he'd met along his route, women who just couldn't resist the fatal charms of Jim Oliphant. I figured that most of them were lies. First of all, there could not have been that many frustrated housewives in Medford, and secondly, even though Old Jim might be considered a good-looking guy, he was dumb as a post, and a borderline alcoholic. And while I was thinking all this, damn if he didn't start up with another whopper about his amorous adventures on the meter trail.

"Had a little treat waiting for me on my rounds last week," he said, turning to his companion. The voice came out thin and whiny, like he was talking through his nose.

"Oh, yeah?" Cecil said. "What kind of treat?"

"The best kind," said Oliphant, taking a swig from the bottle. "The kind that only a woman can give you."

"Uh-huh, and who was the woman?"

"I ain't inclined to say, right now, but if I told you, you wouldn't believe it."

"Hell," Jackson snorted. "I probably wouldn't believe you anyway." Gazing at his fellow hunter, he added, "If you'd laid as many women on that route as you say, you'd never get a day's work done."

Jim gave a wide yawn and murmured, "Whatever you say, Cecil."

I watched Cecil Jackson take a final drag from his cigarette and flip the smoking butt into the dry grass. Go ahead, I thought. Might as well set the woods on fire. He watched the smoke, rising from the grass, then glanced sideways at his partner. Oliphant's lips twitched in a smile and he started humming a Willie Nelson song. This went on for awhile, till, thankfully, Jackson interrupted him.

"All right," he exclaimed, "I know you're dying to tell the tale, so go ahead and get it out of your system."

"What tale?" came the innocent query.

Cecil sighed and stretched his legs out to the front. "The one about your latest conquest," he sneered," or your latest daydream."

Old Jim wasn't deterred in the least. He turned to look at Cecil, and now the smile was wide and bright. "I still ain't saying who," he stated. "I ain't even saying where, but she's fine as wine and she lives on my route."

"Of course," responded his friend. "They all live on your route."

"Where else," said Oliphant. "I don't visit honkytonks and I'm home with my wife every night."

"Okay, just get on with it."

Oliphant took another pull on the bottle and stuck it in his coat pocket. "Last Tuesday, I was reading the meters on the west side of town, when I came up to my house."

"I didn't think the city would let you read your own meter?"

"Not where I *live*, dummy. I just think of it as *my house* because of the woman inside. She is break your heart beautiful, and she's alone every day." Jim swatted a wasp away, and gave his partner a bashful look. "See, sometimes I kinda imagine I'm her husband, and I live there, too."

There was an uncomfortable silence until Cecil finally broke it. "Don't she have a real husband?"

"Oh, yeah, but he goes to work early, comes home late, and eats lunch in town."

"Sounds like you did some spying?"

"Well, let's just say I did a little investigating."

"Where's he work?" asked Jackson.

Oliphant gave him a quick look. "Nice try, Cecil, but you ain't gonna trick nothing out of me. I got too much respect for that woman to ever let anybody know who she is."

Jackson peered at Oliphant and said, "First time I ever heard you use that word about a woman. How'd you come to feel that way about her?"

"I don't know, except that she was so honest about it."

"Honest about what?"

"About what she wanted," answered Jim, "and how she wanted it right then."

"Uh-huh! You know, my man, all your cock stories are starting to sound alike."

Oliphant sat up straight and his voice grew louder. "Ain't no cock story, Cecil, and I shouldn't even be telling you about it. Now, you want to hear this thang or not?"

Jackson leaned his head back against the tree, nudged his friend, and said in a soothing voice, "Okay, Jimbo, tell away."

"Well, it was last Tuesday, like I said, 'bout the middle of the afternoon. I parked my pickup in front of her house and headed up the sidewalk. I was about to go around to where the meter was, when she came out on the front porch. I'd seen her there before, sitting in a rocker and reading, but she'd never looked up from her book. This time, though, she stood there staring at me. She was wearing a short, flimsy dress, and I swear, I just couldn't take my eyes off those legs. They were so damn perfect, I kept staring at them, even after she spoke to me. I finally realized she'd said 'hello' and I looked her in the face. Then she said something that made my throat go dry."

"What was that?" asked Jackson, finally showing some interest.

"She said, 'Can you come inside, for a moment?' I mean it was just like that, one hello and an *in*vite into her house. Hell, I just took a deep breath and followed her through the door. She went ahead of me into the bedroom and walked over to the window. I watched her close the curtains and turn to face me. Then she slipped that dress up over her head."

"Don't tell me. She didn't have anything on underneath."

"Not a stitch," said Oliphant. "So there she stood, with her feet set apart and her hands on her hips, and partner, that bare body of hers would make a Las Vegas show girl ashamed to come out on the stage. It just didn't have a flaw. Again, it took a minute for me to realize she was talking to me."

"Promise me you won't ever tell anybody about this. It'll never happen again, but it will happen today if you swear you'll never say a word."

"I took a big swallow and said, 'I swear, I'll never say a word.' Then I got naked, too, and we both fell onto the bed. It didn't take long for her, or me either, but pardner, it was the greatest I've ever had."

Cecil gave him a narrow look and said, "Kinda forgot your promise, didn't you?"

"Whaddaya mean?" asked Oliphant.

"You swore to her that you wouldn't tell anybody. And now, you're telling me."

"Well, hell, Cecil. I was swearing I wouldn't tell *on* her, and I haven't. You still don't have the slightest idea who she is."

"Hmm, that ain't exactly what you told her. That is, if the woman even exits. Hell, Jim, you caint even give me one hint about her looks."

"I told you she was beautiful."

"There's a hundred beautiful women in Medford."

Oliphant stood up and brushed some dead leaves from his trousers. Jackson arose, also, and both men hefted their rifles. I remained motionless, afraid they'd look up and see their audience.

"I ain't gonna describe her," said Oliphant, "because, if I did, you'd know right away who she is. But I'll tell you one little thing about her that only her husband might know."

"Oh, yeah? And what little thing is that?"

"She has a birthmark," said Jim Oliphant.

His buddy shrugged and said, "So?"

Oliphant answered in a voice gone dreamy and distant. "It looked like a diamond, a deep red diamond, set next to her golden fur."

I watched the two men head up the trail, Oliphant's mouth still working, the nasal voice droning. But I could no longer make out the words, or hear any sound at all for the roaring in my ears. I sat on my tree stand for a very long time, my brain and body numb to everything around me. Then I felt myself pitching forward and grabbed a nearby limb to keep from falling. After a moment, I let my rifle drop to the ground and climbed down after it. I stood beneath the deer stand for the longest time, trying to think, trying to figure out what to do, feeling like the last human on earth.

Finally, I leaned my back against the tree trunk and slowly slid down it until I was sitting in the same place Jim and Cecil had sat. There was really nothing I needed to do right now. I would just sit here for awhile. Maybe I'd sit here the rest of the day, and then I would sit here through the night. Naomi would wonder where I was, but that really didn't matter anymore. Right now, nothing seemed to matter much at all.

AT THE END

"The only truly dead are those who have been forgotten."
—Jewish saying

Supper For The Dead

LaGrange, Arkansas rests at the bottom of a western slope on Crowley's Ridge, and just above the town, atop the Ridge itself, lays LaGrange Cemetery.

It is old, this cemetery, and bespeaks its age with hand carved and crudely lettered headstones. Modern stones stand here, too, and fresh dark earth, neatly mounded in front of a few, speaks of new deaths and more replenishment for this ancient ground. Tall pine trees grow between the graves and a constant wind blows through them, making the pine needles tremble and quiver with its passing. And this graveyard wind is the whispering voice of that place, a voice of the old and the new and the eternal.

Tonight, there are people in LaGrange who look up at the tombstones, shining in the moonlight, for a personal view of their own eternity, staring out of darkness at the gleaming stones. And the graveyard wind whispers its message in their ears, meaningless to them while they live.

They have come to honor their dead with an annual supper, making drives from the neighboring towns of Forrest City and Marianna and Helena. Proceeds from the supper will go toward the upkeep of the graveyard on the hill. The chill of November is upon them as they huddle together in front of a wooden building that was once a general store. Warm light streams through the windows and falls on the crude front porch. The entrance remains locked and the crowd stares through the glass at the workers inside and an impatient murmur goes up. Their appetites are as sharp as the night air and they can smell the food. The food is chitterlings and barbecue. It has always been chitterlings and barbecue with side dishes of coleslaw and potato salad.

Presently, the front door opens and the crowd moves inside. Kathy Huffstedler stands behind a table and a cash box. She collects ten dollars from each person and gives them a smiling thank you. Kathy is here for her father, Otto Huffstedler, who lies buried on the hill. She is also here for her sister, Anne, lying beside the father. They both died together in the wreckage of a car.

Sam Rutledge presses ten dollars into Kathy's hand and moves over to the food. A mound of barbecued chicken stands steaming before him. The slaw and potato salad, plus a wicker basket filled with warm rolls, are set to one side. He takes some of each and steps in front of the chitterlings.

Half have been boiled and they simmer in an iron pot. The rest are fried and lie on a great flat platter. Both dishes resemble nothing so much as what they are, washed out hog entrails. Their aroma enforces this identity. Sam takes a couple of the fried ones (those boiled are strictly for the purists) and walks to a table in the corner. The woman who shared his days lies in the graveyard on the hill. A ruptured appendix killed her. When it happened, they lived fifty miles from the nearest doctor. There was really nothing to be done. Her name was Iris. On her tombstone it reads:

Iris Rutledge
Born January 13, 1959, Died March 18, 1989
Beloved Wife of Sam Rutledge

The old wooden building begins to fill up with people. More stand in a line which reaches out on the porch and down the front steps and halfway across the dirt yard. They file by Kathy, fill up their plates, and find seats at the rough-hewn tables. Bare light bulbs hang from the ceiling by their own electric cords. Occasionally they are bumped and they swing to and fro and cast dark, darting shadows on the wooden walls. The crowd moves through their circles of light while the plank floor creaks and dust drifts up from the timbers. Motes of dust swirl round the light bulbs. A clanking of dishes can be heard, along with sudden laughter and lively talk.

All who are here have someone who is buried on the hill.

Cole Barton leans back and takes a long drink of iced tea. He is here for his younger brother, a suicide. Gene Barton tried to climb a fence with a shotgun under his arm. It discharged and tore part of his leg away. The doctor wanted to amputate, but Gene wouldn't let him and finally gangrene set in. A few days afterward, Cole found his little brother in the barn with that same shotgun by his side and a massive wound in his chest. The older brother took off his coat, thought for a moment, then gently laid the garment over Gene's ruined leg.

Bobby Williams is here with his wife and two of their three sons. The other son lies sleeping on the hill.

Maggie Wheeler has reached the age of eighty-three. Last year, she became a widow and buried John Wheeler on the hill.

Lucy Mangum's husband, Floyd, tried many occupations and failed at all of them and became an alcoholic and that killed him and he lies sleeping on the hill.

Ronald Davis had a twin. His name was Donald. They were born five minutes apart. Ronald is now eight years older than his brother, who ceased to age when they took him to the hill.

Stuart Simpson works a farm. His father taught him how, and once a month Stuart visits his father on the hill. Often, he tells his father what the weather is like. That's very important to a farmer.

We are here, they say, in tribute to those buried on the hill.

From a corner of the room comes the sound of a guitar being tuned, followed by the long drawn out note of a bow moving across a fiddle string. Then comes the plunk, plunk of a banjo. Those who have finished eating amble over and watch the three men get ready to play. They begin with a fast one, called "Under the Double Eagle," and everyone claps along in time. Then they do the "Tennessee Waltz" and a few couples clear a space next to the musicians and begin to dance. Next, they play a hoedown and then more slow ones and the songs go on and on into the night. Finally, the little band closes with "Auld Lang Syne" and there's no other sound save the guitar and the banjo and the mournful violin.

All thoughts are on the honored guests, all resting on the hill.

The night has grown older and the survivors finally exit the building and head for their cars. A few glance up at the tombstones, still shining under a cold moon. Soon afterward, the final car disappears into the distance and the last light in LaGrange blinks out. A bank of clouds is flowing in to drift across the moon.

And darkness covers all who lie sleeping and all who lie dead.

Presently, the Graveyard Wind flows down from its home on the hill and washes across the silent town. It lifts withered leaves from the empty streets and sends them whirling through the night. They soar through the air, flying against bedroom windowpanes and tapping like skeletal fingers on the glass.

The Wind climbs and turns and swoops toward the place of the Supper, where it causes a shutter to bang once and once again against the old store building. Swirling round and round the building, it moans out its message and bestows a fond embrace.

Death is not the end moans the Graveyard Wind.

And blows back up the hill.

~End~

About the Author

H. R. Williams grew up on Crowley's Ridge, a line of hills and a geographical region that figures in many of his stories. He was a paratrooper in the 101st Airborne Division and held about a thousand jobs (slight exaggeration) before coming to the conclusion that his only talent lay in writing.

Since then, his short fiction and essays have appeared in a wide assortment of national magazines and have won numerous awards.

Mr. Williams' western novel, *Harris: The Return of the Gunfighter,* was sold to Treble Heart Books and published in August of 2007. His mystery novel, *The Whiskey Killing,* represented by the August Agency in New York City, was purchased by Thomson-Gale Publications and released in February of 2008. Prior to its release, *The Whiskey Killing* was awarded a First Prize by the National League of American PEN Women.

Both novels are under consideration for movies by Fred Specktor and the Creative Artists Agency in Los Angeles.